T0090867

THE CAPTAIN AND THE ENEMY

Graham Greene was born in 1904. After finishing his studies at Balliol College, Oxford, he worked for four years as sub-editor on the *Times*. He established his reputation with his fourth novel, *Stamboul Train*. In 1935 he made a journey across Liberia, described in *Journey Without Maps*, and on his return was appointed film critic of the *Spectator*. In 1926 he had been received into the Roman Catholic Church and visited Mexico in 1938 to report on the religious persecution there. As a result he wrote *The Lawless Roads* and, later, his famous novel *The Power and the Glory*.

Brighton Rock was published in 1938, and in 1940 he became literary editor of the *Spectator*. The next year he undertook work for the Foreign Office and was stationed in Sierra Leone from 1941 to 1943. This later produced his novel *The Heart of the Matter*, set in West Africa. Other novels include *The End of the Affair*, *The Quiet American*, *Travels with My Aunt*, and *The Honorary Consul*.

As well as his many novels, Graham Greene wrote several collections of short stories, four travel books, six plays, two books of autobiography, two of biography, and four books for children. He also contributed hundreds of essays and film and book reviews, some of which appear in a collection entitled *Reflections*. Many of his novels and short stories have been filmed, and *The Third Man* was written as a film treatment. Graham Greene was a member of the Order of Merit and a Companion of Honour.

Graham Greene died in April 1991. Among the many people who paid tribute to him on his death were Kingsley Amis: 'He will be missed all over the world. Until today, he was our greatest living novelist'; Alec Guinness: 'He was a great writer who spoke brilliantly to a whole generation. He was almost prophet-like with a surprising humility'; and William Golding: 'Graham Greene was in a class by himself. . . . He will be read and remembered as the ultimate chronicler of twentieth-century man's consciousness and anxiety.'

THE CAPTAIN AND THE ENEMY

GRAHAM GREENE

"WILL YOU BE SURE TO KNOW
THE GOOD SIDE FROM THE BAD,
THE CAPTAIN FROM THE ENEMY?"
George A. Birmingham

PENGUIN BOOKS

PENGUIN BOOKS
Published by the Penguin Group
Penguin Putnam Inc., 375 Hudson Street,
New York, New York 10014, U.S.A.
Penguin Books Ltd, 27 Wrights Lane, London W8 5TZ, England
Penguin Books Australia Ltd, Ringwood, Victoria, Australia
Penguin Books Canada Ltd, 10 Alcorn Avenue,
Toronto, Ontario, Canada M4V 3B2
Penguin Books (N.Z.) Ltd, 182–190 Wairau Road,
Auckland 10, New Zealand

Penguin Books Ltd, Registered Offices:
Harmondsworth, Middlesex, England

First published in Great Britain by Reinhardt Books 1988
First published in the United States of America by Viking Penguin,
a division of Penguin Books USA Inc. 1988
Published in Penguin Books 1989
This edition published in Penguin Books 1999

Quote by George Birmingham reprinted by permission
of A. P. Watt Ltd on behalf of Althea Hannay.

LIBRARY OF CONGRESS CATALOGING IN PUBLICATION DATA
Greene, Graham, 1904–91.
The captain and the enemy / Graham Greene.
p.   cm.
ISBN 0 14 01.8855 X
I. Title.
[PR6013.R44C28   1989]
823'.912—dc19   89–3740

Set in Sabon

For Y
with all the memories
we share of nearly thirty
years

No character in this book is based on a living person. One cannot call all one's characters by letters of the alphabet. Mr Quigly of this novel bears no resemblance in character or spelling to a Mr Quigley whom I encountered for a few minutes in Washington ten years ago. For some unknown reason the name haunted me and I wrote in *Getting to Know the General* 'I can make use of that name one day in God knows what story.' Many Quigleys wrote to me kindly after that, but this Quigly is my own and unrelated to any of them.

PART

I

I

(1)

I am now in my twenty-second year and yet the only birthday which I can clearly distinguish among all the rest is my twelfth, for it was on that damp and misty day in September I met the Captain for the first time. I can still remember the wetness of the gravel under my gym shoes in the school quad and how the blown leaves made the cloisters by the chapel slippery as I ran recklessly to escape from my enemies between one class and the next. I slithered and came to an abrupt halt while my pursuers went whistling away, because there in the middle of the quad stood our formidable headmaster talking to a tall man in a bowler hat, a rare sight already at that date, so that he looked a little like an actor in costume – an impression not so far wrong, for I never saw him in a bowler hat again. He carried a walking-stick over his shoulder at the slope like a soldier with a rifle. I had no idea who he might be, nor, of course, did I know how he had won me the previous night, or so he was to claim, in a backgammon game with my father.

I slid so far that I landed on my knees at the two men's feet, and when I picked myself up the headmaster was glaring at me from under his heavy eyebrows. I heard him say, 'I *think* this is the one you want – Baxter Three. Are you Baxter Three?'

'Yes, sir,' I said.

The man, whom I would never come to know by any

more permanent name than the Captain, said, 'What does Three indicate?'

'He is the youngest of three Baxters,' the headmaster said, 'but not one of them is related by blood.'

'That puts me in a bit of a quandary,' the Captain said. 'For which of them is the Baxter I want? The Christian name, unlikely as it may sound, is Victor. Victor Baxter — the names don't pair very well.'

'We have little occasion here for Christian names. Are you called Victor Baxter?' the headmaster inquired of me sharply.

'Yes, sir,' I said after some hesitation, for I was reluctant to admit to a name which I had tried unsuccessfully to conceal from my fellows. I knew very well that Victor for some obscure reason was one of the unacceptable names, like Vincent or Marmaduke.

'Well then, I suppose that this is the Baxter you want, sir. Your face needs washing, boy.'

The stern morality of the school prevented me from telling the headmaster that it had been quite clean until my enemies had splashed it with ink. I saw the Captain regarding me with brown, friendly and what I came to learn later from hearsay, unreliable eyes. He had such deep black hair that it might well have been dyed and a long thin nose which reminded me of a pair of scissors left partly ajar, as though his nose was preparing to trim the military moustache just below it. I thought that he winked at me, but I could hardly believe it. In my experience grown-ups did not wink, except at each other.

'This gentleman is an old boy, Baxter,' the headmaster said, 'a contemporary of your father's he tells me.'

'Yes, sir.'

'He has asked permission to take you out this afternoon. He has brought me a note from your father, and as today is a half holiday, I see no reason why I shouldn't give my consent, but you must be back at your house by six. He understands that.'

'Yes, sir.'

'You can go now.'

I turned my back and began to make for the classroom where I was overdue.

'I meant go with this gentleman, Baxter Three. What class do you miss?'

'Divvers, sir.'

'He means Divinity,' the headmaster told the Captain. He glared at the door across the quad from which wild sounds were emerging, and he swept his black gown back over his shoulder. 'From what I can hear you will miss little by not attending.' He began to make great muffled strides towards the door. His boots – he always wore boots – made no more sound than carpet slippers.

'What's going on in there?' the Captain asked.

'I think they are slaying the Amalekites,' I said.

'Are you an Amalekite?'

'Yes.'

'Then we'd better be off.'

He was a stranger, but I felt no fear of him at all. Strangers were not dangerous. They had no such power as the headmaster or my fellow pupils. A stranger is not a permanency. One can easily shed a stranger. My mother had died a few years back – I could not even then have said how long before; time treads at quite a different pace when one is a child. I had seen her on her deathbed, pale and calm, like a figure on a tomb, and when she hadn't responded to my formal kiss on her forehead, I realized with no great shock of grief that she had gone to join the angels. At that time, before I went to school, my only fear was of my father who, according to what my mother told me, had long since attached himself to the opposing party up there where she had gone. 'Your father is a devil,' she was very fond of telling me, and her eyes would lose their habitual boredom and light suddenly up for a moment like a gas cooker.

My father, I do remember that, came to the funeral dressed top to toe in black; he had a beard which went well with the suit, and I looked for the tail under his coat, but I couldn't perceive one, although this did little to reassure me. I had not seen him very often before the day of the funeral, nor after, for he seldom came to my home, if you could call the flat in a semidetached house named The Laurels near Richmond Park where I began to live after my mother's death, a home. It was at the buffet party which followed the funeral that I now believe he plied my mother's sister with sherry until she promised to provide a shelter for me during the school holidays.

My aunt was quite an agreeable but very boring woman and understandably she had never married. She too referred to my father as the Devil on the few occasions when she spoke of him, and I began to feel a distinct respect for him, even though I feared him, for to have a devil in the family was after all a kind of distinction. An angel one had to take on trust, but the Devil in the words of my prayer book 'roamed the world like a raging lion', which made me think that perhaps it was for that reason my father spent so much more time in Africa than in Richmond. Now after so many years have passed

I begin to wonder whether he was not quite a good man in his own way, something which I would hesitate to say of the Captain who had won me from him at backgammon, or so he said.

'Where shall we go now?' the Captain asked me. 'I hadn't expected you to be released as easily as all that. I thought there would be a lot of papers to sign – there are nearly always papers to be signed in my experience. It's too early for lunch,' he added.

'It's nearly twelve,' I said. Bread, jam and tea at eight always left me hungry.

'My appetite only begins at one, but my thirst is always there at least half an hour before – however twelve is good enough for me – but you are too young to take into a bar.' He looked me up and down. 'You would certainly never pass. Why, you are even small for your age.'

'We could go for a walk,' I suggested without enthusiasm because walks were a compulsory feature of school life on Sundays and often entailed the slaughter of some Amalekites.

'Where to?'

'There's the High Street or the Common or the Castle.'

'I seem to remember on the way from the station that I saw a pub called the Swiss Cottage.'

'Yes. By the canal.'

'You could be trusted, I suppose, to stay outside while I swallowed a gin and tonic. I shan't be long doing that.'

All the same he was away for nearly half an hour and I think now with the wisdom of the years that he must have swallowed at least three.

I loitered by a timber yard close by and stared at the green weeds of the canal. I felt very happy. I was not puzzled at all by the Captain's arrival, I accepted it. It had just happened like a fine day between two weeks of rain. It was there because it was there. I wondered whether it would be possible to build a raft out of the planks in the yard and float it down towards the sea. A canal of course was not a river, but yet surely a canal would have to end in a river, for we lived – so I understood from my geography classes – on an island and a river always came eventually to the sea. A sail might be made out of my shirt, but there was also the question of provisions for a long journey . . .

I was deep in thought when the Captain came out of the Swiss Cottage and asked me abruptly, 'Have you any money?'

I counted out what was left of my last week's pocket-money which was always paid by my housemaster on Sundays – perhaps because on that day the shops were all closed and out of the range of temptation; even the school tuckshop was not open on Sunday. He little realized what an opportunity Sunday gave for complicated financial operations, for the payment of debts, for the arrangement of forced loans, the calculations of interest, and for the marketing of unwanted possessions.

'Three and threepence halfpenny,' I told the Captain. It was not so small a sum in those days before the metric system when money was still relatively stable. The Captain went back into the pub and I began to consider what foreign coinage I would need to take with me on my voyage. I came to the conclusion that pieces of eight would probably prove the most practical.

'The landlord had no change,' the Captain explained when he returned.

It did occur to me then that he might himself have run short of money, but when he said, 'And now for a good lunch at The Swan,' I knew I must be wrong. Even my aunt had never taken me to The Swan: she would always arrive at the school with home-made sandwiches wrapped in greaseproof paper and with a thermos full of hot milk. 'I don't trust meals cooked by strangers,' she had often told me, and she would add, 'and from the prices they charge in restaurants, you can tell that they are not honest meals.'

The bar of The Swan was crowded when we arrived and the Captain installed me at a table in an annexe which apparently counted as a restaurant so that the law allowed me to sit there. I could watch him exchanging a few words with the landlord and his precise and authoritative voice carried through all the rumble-tumble of the bar. 'Two single rooms for the night,' I heard him say. For a moment I wondered who was going to join him, but my mind drifted off to more interesting things, for never before had I even been in sight of a bar and I was fascinated. Everyone standing there had so much to say and everyone seemed to be in a good humour. I thought of the raft and the long voyage I had planned, and it seemed to me that I had arrived at the other end of the world, in the romantic city of Valparaiso, and that I was carousing with foreign sailors who had sailed the Seven Seas – true, they all wore collars and ties, but perhaps one had to dress up a little if one went ashore in Valparaiso. My imagination was aided by a small barrel on the bar which I supposed must contain rum, and a sword without a scabbard – undoubtedly a cutlass – which was hanging as a decoration above the landlord's head.

'A double gin and tonic at the table,' the Captain was saying, 'and something fizzy for the boy.'

I thought with admiration how he was completely at home in a place like this, he was at ease in Valparaiso. The tobacco smoke, driven by a draught from an open door, blew around my head and I sniffed up the fumes with pleasure. The Captain told the landlord, 'You'll remember, won't you, that you've got my suitcase behind the bar? If you would just send it up to my room. I and the boy will take a walk after lunch. Or tell me – is there a suitable movie?'

'The only film that's on,' the landlord said, 'is a pretty old one. *The Daughter of Tarzan* it's called, and I wouldn't know if it's suitable or not. There's a girl who makes love with an ape I believe . . .'

'Is there a matinée?'

'Yes, today's Saturday, so there'll be one at two-thirty.'

The Captain came to me at the table. He picked up the menu and told me, 'Some smoked salmon, I think, for a start. Afterwards would you rather have a pork chop or a lamb cutlet?' The landlord himself brought us what I supposed was the gin and tonic and a fizzy drink which proved to be orangeade. After he had gone the Captain gave me a short lecture. 'Remember that it's never too late to learn from a man like myself who has been around. If you are a bit short of cash – which will often happen when you are my age – never drink at the bar, unless you've booked a room first, for otherwise they want their money straightaway. That orange fizz and my gin go on the price of the meal and the cost of that goes on the price of the room.' What he said meant nothing at all to me then. It was only later that I appreciated the Captain's foresight and saw that he was trying in his own way to prepare me for a new life.

It was a very good meal we had, though the salmon made me thirsty, and the Captain, seeing me look a little wistfully at my empty glass, ordered me another orangeade. 'We'll have to take a walk,' he said, 'if only to let the gas escape.' I was beginning to lose some of the awe I had felt for him and I ventured on a question. 'Are you a sea captain?' But no, he said, he didn't care for the sea, he was an army man. Remembering his loan from me at the Swiss Cottage I waited with some anxiety to see if he would have trouble in paying, but all he did was to take the bill and write his name on it with a number which he explained to me was the number of his room. I noticed that he wrote 'J. Victor (Capt.)'. It struck me as an odd coincidence that his surname was the same as my Christian one, but at the same time it gave me a comfortable feeling, a feeling that at last I had found a relative whom I could like – one who was neither an angel nor a devil nor an aunt.

After our very good lunch the Captain began to talk to the landlord about the dinner which we would be taking next. 'We'll want it early,' he said. 'A boy of his age ought to be in bed by eight.'

'I can see you know how to bring up a child.'

'I've had to learn the hard way. You see, his mother's dead.'

'Ah! Have a brandy, sir, on the house. It's not an easy thing for a man to play the mother's part.'

'I never refuse a good offer,' the Captain said, and a minute later they were clicking glasses together over the bar. It did occur to me that I had never seen anyone less like a mother than the Captain.

'Time, gentlemen, time,' the landlord called and added in a confidential tone to the Captain, 'Of course it doesn't apply to you, sir, you being a guest in the hotel. Can I give your nipper another orangeade?'

'Better not,' the Captain said. 'Too much gas you know.' I was to discover as time went on that the Captain had a strong disinclination for gas – a sentiment which I shared, for in the dormitory at night there were too many of my companions who liked to show off the vigour of their farts.

'About that early dinner,' the Captain said.

'We don't usually serve a hot meal before eight. But if you wouldn't mind something tasty and cold . . .'

'I prefer it.'

'Shall we say a bit of cold chicken and a slice of ham . . . ?'

'And perhaps a little green salad?' the Captain suggested. 'A growing boy needs a bit of green – or so his mother used to say. For me – well, I've lived too long in the tropics where a salad can mean dysentery and death . . . However if you have a bit of that apple tart left . . .'

'And a bit of cheese to go with it?' the landlord suggested with a sort of enthusiasm for good works.

'Not for me, not at night,' the Captain said, 'gassy again. Well, we'll be getting along now. I'll take a look at the pictures outside the cinema. *Tarzan's Daughter* you said, didn't you? One can generally judge from the pictures outside if a film's suitable for a child. If it's not, we'll just go for a walk, and I might slip in myself for the evening performance when the boy's safe in bed.'

'You turn left out of the door, and then it's just across the road a hundred yards down.'

'We'll be seeing you,' the Captain replied and we went out, but to my surprise we turned sharp right.

'The cinema's the other way,' I said.

'We are not going to the cinema.'

I was disappointed, and I tried to reassure him. 'Lots of the day boys have been to *Tarzan's Daughter*.'

The Captain halted. He said, 'I'll give you a free choice. We'll go and see *Tarzan's Daughter* if you insist and then back you must go to – what did that pompous old ass call it? – your "house", or else we don't go to the film and you don't go to your house.'

'Where do I go?'

'There's a good train to London at three o'clock.'

'You mean we can go all the way to London. But when do we come back?'

'We don't come back – unless of course you want to see *Tarzan's Daughter*.'

'I don't want to see *Tarzan's Daughter* that much.'

'Well then . . . Is this the way to the station, boy?'

'Yes, but you ought to know.'

'Why the hell should I know? I took a different route this morning.'

'But you're an old boy, the headmaster said.'

'This is the first time I've ever seen the bloody town.'

He put a hand on my shoulder and I could feel kindness in the touch. He said, 'When you get to know me better, boy, you'll realize that I don't always tell the exact truth. Any more than you do, I expect.'

'But I always get found out.'

'Ah, you'll have to learn to tell a lie properly. What's the good of a lie if it's seen through? When I tell a lie no one can tell it from the gospel truth. Sometimes I can't even tell it myself.'

We walked down what was called Castle Street, which led us past the school, and I dreaded to think that he might prove to be wrong in his choice and that the headmaster would come sailing out of the quad with his gown spread like the sail of a pinnace and catch both me and the Captain out, but all was as quiet as quiet.

Outside the Swiss Cottage the Captain hesitated for a moment, but the door was shut – the bar had closed. A child screamed at us from one of the painted barges on the canal – the barge children always screamed at the schoolchildren. It was like cat and dog – the enmity was noisy but never came as far as a bite. I said, 'What about your bag at the hotel?'

'There's nothing in it but a couple of bricks.'

'Bricks?'

'Yes, bricks.'

'You are going to leave them behind?'

'Why not? One can always lay one's hand on a few bricks when required and the bag's an old one. Old bags with a few labels stuck on inspire confidence. Especially labels from foreign parts. A new bag looks stolen.'

I was still puzzled. After all I knew enough about life to realize that, even if he possessed a return ticket, he would have to pay for mine. All my money had gone at the Swiss Cottage to help pay for his gin and tonics. And then there was the lunch we had eaten – a feast, there was no meal in my memory that I could compare with it We had nearly reached the station when I said, 'But you haven't paid for our lunch, have you?'

'Bless you, boy. I signed for it. What more do you expect me to do?'

'Is your name really Victor?'

'Oh, sometimes it's one thing and sometimes it's another. It wouldn't be much fun, would it, always carrying the same name from birth till death. Baxter now. It's not what I'd call a beautiful name. You've had it a good many years now, haven't you?'

'Twelve.'

'Too long. We'll think of a better name for you on the train. I don't like Victor either if it comes to that.'

'But what shall I call *you*?'

'Just call me Captain unless I tell you different. There might come a time when I'd like to be addressed as Colonel – or Dad too might prove convenient – in certain situations. Though I'd rather avoid it. I'll let you know when a certain situation does arise, but I think you'll soon pick things up for yourself. I can see that you are an intelligent boy.'

We entered the station and he had no difficulty at all in producing the cash for my ticket – 'Third class half single to Euston.' We had a compartment to ourselves and that gave me the courage to ask him, 'I thought you had no money.'

'What gave you that idea?'

'Well, there's all that lunch we had and you just signed a paper and you did seem to need some money too at the Swiss Cottage.'

'Ah,' he said, 'that's another point you'll have to learn. It isn't that I'm without money, but I like to preserve it for essentials.'

The Captain settled in a corner and began to smoke a cigarette. Twice he looked at his watch. It was a very slow train, and whenever we stopped at a station, I could feel a certain tension stretching from the window seat opposite me. The lean dark Captain reminded me of a coiled spring which had once snapped on my fingers when I was taking an old clock to pieces. At Willesden I asked him, 'Are you afraid?'

'Afraid?' he asked in a puzzled way as though I had employed a word that he would have to look up in a dictionary.

'Scared,' I translated for him.

'Boy,' he said, 'I'm never scared. I'm on my guard – that's different.'

'Yes.'

As an Amalekite I understood the distinction, and I felt that perhaps I was getting to know the Captain a little bit better.

(2)

At Euston we took a taxi for what seemed to me a very long ride – I couldn't tell in those days whether we were travelling east or west or north or south. I could only suppose that this taxi ride was one of the essentials for which the Captain had kept his money. All the same I was surprised that when we arrived at our destination – a certain number in a dusty crescent where the dustbins had not been emptied – he waited for the taxi to go, following it with his eyes until it was out of sight, and then began to walk a long way back on the route we had come. He must have felt a question in my silence and my obedience because he answered it, though unsatisfactorily. 'Exercise is good for the two of us,' he told me. He added, 'I take a bit of exercise whenever I get the chance.'

There was nothing I could do but accept his explanation, and I think that in some way the readiness of my acquiescence worried him just a little, for, as we strolled silently along side by side, taking this turning and then that, he began occasionally to break the silence with a too obvious attempt at conversation.

He said, 'I don't suppose you remember your mother?'

'Oh, yes, I do, but she's been dead, you know, an awfully long time.'

'Yes, that's true. Your father told me . . .' but he never said what it was that my father had told him.

We must have walked at least a quarter of a mile before he spoke again. 'Do you miss her?'

Children, I think, lie usually from fear, and there seemed to be nothing in his questions to make me afraid of the Captain. 'Not really,' I said.

He gave a grunt, which with my limited experience I took to be a note of disapproval – or perhaps of disappointment. Our footsteps on the pavement measured out the long length of the silence between us.

'I hope you aren't going to be difficult,' he said to me at last.

'Difficult?'

'I mean I hope you are quite a normal boy. She'd be disappointed if you weren't a normal boy.'

'I don't understand.'

'I would say a normal boy would miss his mother.'

'I never knew her very well,' I said. 'There wasn't time.'

He gave a prolonged sigh. 'I hope you'll do,' he said. 'I hope to God you'll do.'

Again he walked along in silent thought and then he asked me, 'Are you tired?'

'No,' I said, but I said it only to please him – I *was* tired. I would have liked to know just how much further we had still to go.

The Captain said, 'She's a marvellous woman. You'll know that as soon as you see her if you've any judgement about women – but how could you have any at your age? Of course you'll have to be patient with her. Make allowances. She's suffered a great deal.'

The word 'suffer' meant to me at that time the splashes of ink upon my face which still remained there (the Captain, unlike the headmaster, didn't notice things like that), the visible sign of being an Amalekite, an outcast.

The reason I had become an outcast at school was not at all clear to me – it was partly, perhaps, because my name had leaked out, but I think it was connected too with my aunt and her sandwiches, the fact that she never took me to a restaurant as parents always seemed to do when they visited their children. Someone had spied on us, I suppose, as we sat beside the canal and ate the sandwiches, drinking not even orangeade or Coca-Cola but hot milk out of a thermos. Milk! Somebody no doubt had spied the milk. Milk was for babies.

'You understand what I mean?'

I nodded of course – there was nothing else I could do. Perhaps this strange woman would prove to be another Amalekite if it was true that she had suffered. There were three other Amalekites in my house, yet somehow we never combined in our own defence – each one hated the three others for being an Amalekite. An Amalekite, I was beginning to learn, was always a loner.

The Captain said, 'We'll turn around at the end of the street. One just has to be careful.'

After we turned he said, 'I won you fairly.'

I had no idea then what he meant. He added, 'No one in his right mind would try to cheat your father. Anyway you can't cheat easily at backgammon. Your father lost you in a fair game.'

I asked him, 'He's a devil, isn't he?'

'Well, I suppose he could be so described,' the Captain replied, 'but only when he's crossed.' He added, 'You know how it is – but of course you don't, how can you? No child would dare to cross *him*.'

We came finally to a street where some of the houses had been repainted and others were in course of demolition, but there were at least no dustbins. The houses, as I know now, were Victorian, with steps that led down to basements, and attic windows four floors up. There were steps which led to front doors, and some of the doors stood ajar. It was as if the street, which was called Alma Terrace, had not made up its mind whether it was going up in the world or down. We stopped at a house marked 12A because I suppose nobody would have cared to live in number 13. There were five bells beside the door, but someone had stuck Scotch tape over four of them to show that they were not in use.

'Now remember what I told you,' the Captain said. 'Speak gently because she's easily scared,' but I had the impression even then that he was a little scared himself, while he hesitated with his finger near the surviving bell. He rang once, but left his finger on the bell.

'Are you sure she's there?' I asked, for the house had an unlived-in look.

'She doesn't go out much,' he said, 'and besides the dark's coming down. She doesn't like the dark.'

He pressed the bell again with his finger, twice this time, and I heard a movement in the basement, and a light went on. He said, 'I've got a key, but I like to give her warning. Her name's Liza, but I want you to call her mother. Or Mum if you like that better.'

'Why?'

'Oh we'll go into all of that one day. You wouldn't understand now and anyway there isn't time.'

'But she's not my mother.'

'Of course she's not. I'm not saying she is. Mother is just a generic term.'

'What's generic?' I think he took a pleasure in using difficult words – a sort of showing off, but there was more to it than that I learned later.

'Listen. If you aren't happy we can take a train back. You can be at school nearly on time . . . Only a little late . . . I'll come with you and make excuses.'

'You mean I don't have to go back? Not tomorrow?'

'You don't have to go back at all if you don't want to. I'm only asking you.' He had his hand pressed on my shoulder and I could feel it tremble. He seemed frightened, but I wasn't frightened at all. I was no longer an Amalekite. I was freed from fear and I felt prepared for anything when the door in the basement opened.

'I don't want to go back,' I told him.

2

(1)

All the same I was not prepared for the very young and pale face which peered up at us both from the gloom of the basement where a bare globe of a very low watt gave all the light. She didn't look to my eyes like anybody's mother.

'I've brought him,' the Captain said.

'Who?'

'Victor. But I think we'll change all that and call him Jim.'

The possibility had never occurred to me of changing my hated name as easily as that, just by choosing another.

'What on earth have you done?' she asked the Captain, and even I could detect the fear there was in her voice.

He gave me a small push towards the basement steps. 'Go on down,' he said, 'say what I told you to say. And then give her a kiss.'

I took a very small step forward across the lintel and muttered, 'Mother.' It was like the first embarrassing rehearsal I remembered in a school play, in which I had been allotted the most minor part, a play called *Toad of Toad Hall*, but that was before anyone discovered I was an Amalekite. As for the kiss I couldn't manage that.

'What have you done?' she repeated.

'I went down to the school and I brought him out.'

'Just like that?' she said.

'Just like that. You see I had a letter from his father.'

'How on earth . . . ?'

'I won him quite fair and square, I promise you, Liza. You can't cheat at backgammon.'

'You are going to be the death of me,' she said. 'I never meant you to do anything when I said . . . I just thought . . . if only things had been different . . .'

'You might invite us in and give us a cup of tea.'

'Oh, I put the kettle on as soon as you rang. I knew what you'd want.'

In the kitchen she told me rather harshly to sit down. There were two hard chairs and an easy one, so I followed the Captain's example and chose a hard. The kettle was beginning to splutter on the stove. She said, 'I haven't had time to warm the pot.'

'It won't taste any different to me,' the Captain said, I thought with a certain gloom.

'Oh yes, it will.'

They were both strangers to me, and yet already I found that I liked them better than my aunt, not to speak of the headmaster or Mr Harding, my housemaster, or any of the boys I knew. I could tell that in some way they were not at ease with each other and I wanted to help them if it was in my power. I said, 'I had a spiffing lunch.'

'What did he give you?'

'Oh, just a bit of fish,' the Captain said.

'That was only the start,' I told her, 'and the fish was smoked salmon.'

I knew smoked salmon was important because I'd taken a look at the menu and had seen the price they charged. It cost far more than a pork chop.

'How did you pay for it?' she asked. 'You aren't so flush – or you weren't this morning.'

'I gave them that old suitcase you lent me in exchange,' he said.

'That old thing, why it wasn't worth two bob.'

'There were three pairs of socks in it – they had too many holes in them for me to keep – and a brick or two. The landlord was quite content and he even stood me a brandy.'

'Oh, for God's sake,' she said, 'sit down and drink your tea. What do you suppose I'd do if you went to prison?'

'They wouldn't keep me long,' he said. 'Any more than the Huns did, and I had all Germany to walk across then. The Scrubs is nearly next door compared to where I was.'

'And you are more than twenty years older. Listen! Is that someone at the door?'

'It's only your nerves, Liza. No one followed us – I saw to that. Drink your tea and don't worry. You'll see – everything will be hunky-dory.'

'What will they do when he's not back tonight?'

'Well, I left the head man his father's letter, and he'll probably write to him, but I doubt if the old devil will bother to answer. You know very well he doesn't like writing letters, and he won't want to get mixed up in things, and then I suppose the head man might write to the boy's aunt – if he has her address – and she won't know a thing.'

'And after that they'll go to the police. Kidnapped boy. I can just see the headlines.'

'He wasn't kidnapped, Liza. He went away willingly with a friend of his father. The fees are always paid in advance – what do they care? Of course we'll watch the papers for a week or two just in case. You don't *want* to go back to school, do you, Jim?'

'I think I'd rather stay here,' I said, although I wasn't yet quite sure – but it seemed the polite thing to say.

'There you are, you see, Liza, it's as I told you. He's all your own. You're a mother now. A proper mother, Liza.'

'And where shall I put him? We've only the one room.'

'You've got the whole house to choose from. You're the caretaker. You have the keys.'

The day which had begun badly at school certainly ended with a sense of excitement and mystery. We tramped all over the house from the basement to the attic. It was like exploring Africa. Every room when unlocked had its individual secret. The Captain, like a native carrier, supported a pile of blankets. I realized that I had never before visited a whole house. My aunt lived in a flat on the first floor, and she kept away from neighbours.

In those days (I don't know what the custom is now) something was always left in an unoccupied room to enable a landlord to call it furnished, and so I had the choice of three different beds in three different rooms, a dingy sofa in another, and an easy chair big enough to sleep in, but it was the traces of the ancient lodgers who had been expelled, perhaps without notice, or who had moonflit of their own accord, which fascinated me. On the floor of the attic there was a copy of a very old tattered magazine called *Lilliput* over which I lingered long enough for them to notice. 'Would you like to sleep here?' Liza asked, but it was too far away from the basement and human contact, and I said, 'No.'

'Take the mag with you if you want,' the Captain said. 'Finding's keeping – remember that. It's one of the basic laws of human nature.'

We had begun at the top of the house and we trudged on downwards. In another room on a rickety table lay a notebook with lined pages in which somebody had kept accounts. I still remember a few of the entries and they seemed odd to me even then – there were things called penny buns noted down (what can one buy now for a penny, even with a new metric penny?). They seemed much in favour with the owner and there was a note 'Extravagance' marked with an exclamation mark – 'Lunch at the ABC two shillings and threepence.' With a glance at the Captain I put the notebook in my pocket. There were a lot of blank pages, and I thought it might prove useful. I already had literary ambitions which I had not confided either to my aunt or my father. I had read *King Solomon's Mines* four times, and I thought that if I ever went like my father to Africa I would keep a journal of my adventures.

'Why does nobody live here?' I asked them.

'The owners sent all of them away,' Liza said, 'because they want the house pulled down. I'm here to keep out squatters till the owners have got permission.'

She opened another door – it was one of the rooms with beds, and on the lino was a broken comb and a tuft of grey hair. 'An old lady died in this one,' she said, 'she was eighty-nine, and she died on her birthday.' She shut the door again quickly and we went on very much to my relief because of the coincidence. This was my birthday too, though nobody at school knew the fact, the Devil seldom remembered, and my aunt's letter usually arrived several days late with a postal order for five shillings.

I finally chose the room with the sofa because it was

near enough to the basement for me to hear the movements of the other human occupants. There was a small table and a picture on the wall of someone in strange clothes, whom I still for some reason remember was called Mr Lunardi, as he was setting out in a balloon from Richmond Park – it was another odd coincidence seeing that my aunt lived there. The young woman, whom I began to think of as Liza rather than mother, brought up a saucepan to serve as a chamberpot from the basement, and the Captain produced a basin and a cracked jug from a cupboard. 'Soap,' he thought aloud and rummaged further.

I was aware of a yet greater requirement. 'I haven't any pyjamas,' I told him.

'Oh,' Liza said in a tone of utter dismay and she stopped making up the sofa. It was as though a fatal flaw had suddenly been discovered in their plans for my future, and I hastily reassured them. 'It doesn't really matter.' I was afraid they would send me back to the world of the Amalekites for lack of pyjamas. 'I will keep my shirt on and my pants,' I said.

'It wouldn't do,' Liza said. 'It wouldn't be healthy.'

'Don't worry,' the Captain said. He looked at his watch. 'The shops may be closed, but I'll see to it first thing in the morning if they are.'

'I can manage,' I said. 'Really I can manage,' because I thought I knew how short of money he was.

'She wouldn't be happy if you didn't have pyjamas,' he said, and Liza and I listened in silence, as the house door closed behind him.

'It's no good arguing with him,' Liza said, 'when he gets an idea in his head.'

'Pyjamas cost an awful lot of money.'

'He always has money for essentials, or so he says. I don't know how he does it.'

It had been an odd sort of day which had begun so unexpectedly in the school quad. I sat down on the sofa on top of the blankets and Liza sat down beside me.

I said, 'He's an awfully strange man.'

She said, 'He's a very good man,' and of course I didn't know enough to deny it. I certainly felt happier here than there – than all the 'theres', including my aunt's 'there' at Richmond.

'I'm fond of him in my way,' she said, 'and I'm pretty sure he's fond of me – in his way. But sometimes he does such things for me that he frightens me. If I told him I wanted a pearl necklace I bet you he'd turn up with one. Perhaps they wouldn't be real pearls – but they might be all the same and how would I be able to tell? Now you for example . . .'

'He really is a kind man,' I said. 'He gave me two orangeades. And the smoked salmon.'

'Oh he's kind right enough. Yes, he's a kind man. I would never deny that. And you can depend on him – in a way, his way. Those pyjamas – he'll bring them I'm sure. But how will he have got them . . . ?'

Half an hour later I heard the bell ring once and then twice – and I noticed how tensely she waited for the third ring – and there he was, carrying an unwrapped pair of pyjamas. They weren't the pyjamas I would have chosen even at that age – because for some reason I hated the colour orange – and these pyjamas were not only striped with orange but they had oranges on the pockets. (I only liked oranges in the form of orangeade, but even when I drank that I would shut my eyes to hide the colour.)

'Where did you get them?' she asked.

'No difficulty,' he said – as now he would probably have used the phrase 'no problem'.

Is it only with today's eyes that I seemed to see at that moment a certain shiftiness in his? Memory cheats. All I am sure, or half sure, is that he told me, 'Time for bed, Jim.'

'Does he have to be Jim?'

'Any name you want, dear. You choose.'

I'm sure at least that I remember correctly the one word 'dear' which was not in common use either at school or in my aunt's house, or even, I was to find out later, between the two of them.

I went to bed on the sofa in my pants after ruffling the orange pyjamas to disguise the fact.

(2)

I woke next morning to a strange woman's voice calling out the name 'Jim'. I had no idea where I was. I felt under the sofa for the familiar chamberpot, but it wasn't to be found, only a saucepan on the carpet, and in amazement I looked to each side of me expecting to see the wooden divisions which in the school dormitory separated one bed from another, but they were gone. For the first time for years I found myself quite alone – no voices, no heavy breathing, no farts. Only the woman's voice calling from below 'Jim'. Who was 'Jim'? Then I saw the pyjamas on the floor and reluctantly put them on.

As I went down the stairs towards the basement the strange events of the day before came trooping back to mind – I couldn't make sense of them, though I was quite happy because at least I was not back at school, but I felt entirely lost in this new world. I think, perhaps, that, at the age I was then, a boy doesn't give as much importance to happiness as to knowing who he really is. I had been an Amalekite – certainly not a happy Amalekite – but what was of greater importance to me than happiness, I had known my exact position in life. I knew who my enemies were and I knew how to avoid the worst at their hands. But now . . . I pushed open the door at the bottom of the stairs and it wasn't a woman but a pale worried girl, perhaps not much more than twice my age, who confronted me. She said, 'Do you like your egg hard-boiled or soft-boiled?'

I said, 'Soft,' and I added, 'Who's Jim?'

'Don't you remember?' she asked me. 'The Captain said I was to call you Jim. Do you mind the name?'

'Oh no,' I said, 'I'd much rather be Jim than . . .'

'Than what?'

'I'd rather be Jim,' I repeated cagily, for there is a strange importance about names. You can't trust them until you have tried them out. Why should I have been ashamed of Victor and why had I so easily consented to be Jim?

'Where is the Captain?' I asked, only to change the subject.

'Off somewhere,' she said, 'I wouldn't know where,' and she led me into the kitchen and began to boil the water for my egg.

I asked her, 'Does he live here?'

'When he's here,' she said, 'yes, he sort of lives here.' Perhaps the answer had seemed a bit enigmatic even to herself, for she added, 'When you get to know the Captain better, you'll know that it's no good asking him questions. What he wants you to know, he'll tell you.'

'I don't much like these pyjamas,' I said.

'They are a bit on the small side.'

'I don't mean that. I mean the colour – and the oranges.'

'Oh well,' she said, 'I suppose they came first to hand.'

'Perhaps we could change them?'

'We aren't millionaires,' she replied indignantly, and then, 'The Captain's a very kind man. Remember that.'

'It's funny. He has the same name as me.'

'What? Jim?'

'No, my real name.' I added reluctantly, 'Victor,' and watched closely to see if she smiled, but she didn't. She said, 'Oh, I suppose he borrowed it,' and she busied herself with my egg.

'Does he borrow a lot of names?'

'When I knew him first he had a very classy name – Colonel Claridge, but he changed that one pretty quick. He said he couldn't live up to it.'

'What's his name now?'

'You are an inquisitive one, aren't you? It doesn't matter asking *me* questions, but don't go on like that with the Captain. Questions get him worried. He said to me once, "Liza, I seem to have been asked questions all my life long. Give me a rest, won't you," so now I give him a rest, and you must too.'

'But what shall I call him?'

'Call him the Captain like I do. That's a name I hope

he'll always keep.' Suddenly her eyes lighted up, as though she had been brought into a room with a great gleaming Christmas tree hung with baubles and mystery packets. She said, 'There – do you hear it? It's his step on the basement stairs. I'd know it from a thousand, yet he always says I must wait to open up till he rings the third time – a long and two shorts. As though I wouldn't know that it's him before he rings once.'

She was at the door before she finished speaking and sure enough there were three rings – the long ring and the two shorts. Then the door came open and she was greeting him with a mixture of relief and complaint as though he had been away for a year. I watched with curiosity – I suppose I was seeing the complexity of human love for the first time in my life, but what struck me even then was how quickly the expression of it was over. What remained afterwards was shyness in both of them and a kind of fear. She said, 'The boy,' and detached herself.

'Yes, the boy,' he said.

'Will you take an egg?'

'If it's not too much bother. I only came in just to see . . .'

'Yes?'

'To see that it was all right with you and the boy.'

I think that he stayed then and had a bit of breakfast with us, but I don't really remember anything else or whether he was still there when the night came.

(3)

It was about a week after that evening – or was it two or three or even four (time, unlike at school, flowed by uncounted) – before we saw the Captain again, and the circumstances were a little odd. I had learnt a lot during his absence which I had never learnt at school – how to cook sausages and the way you had to spike them before putting them in the pan, and how to break an egg over the pan to make eggs and bacon. I had also become well acquainted with the baker and the butcher, for my adopted mother would often send me out to do the shopping – she had a strange reluctance to leave the house, though every morning she brought herself to go just as far as the corner to buy a newspaper and then she would come scampering back like a mouse to her hole. I didn't know why she bought the paper for she couldn't, in the time which she spent on each one, have read more than the headlines. It is only now I realize that she was expecting every day to read, in large letters, some such headline as Mystery of Missing Schoolboy or Child's Strange Disappearance, and yet when she had finished with a paper she would hide it deep in the waste-paper basket. Once she explained to me, 'The Captain is a very tidy man. He doesn't like old papers littering the place,' but I feel sure that she was really hiding her fears from him because they would have shown a lack of confidence in his wisdom and that doubt of hers might have hurt his pride.

For in his own way he was a very proud man and she had become an essential part of his pride – and a part of his timidity too. Love and fear – fear and love – I know now how inextricably they are linked, but they were both beyond my understanding at the age I was then, and how can I be sure that I really understand them even now?

I was coming out of the baker's with a loaf of bread at the end of that week – if it was only a week – when I found the Captain waiting for me outside. He put his hand in his pocket and stared at a florin and a shilling piece. It took him quite a while to decide on the shilling. He said, 'Go back and get two éclairs: she likes éclairs,' and when I returned, he said, 'Let's take a walk.' Take a walk we did – down several streets, in complete silence. Then the Captain said, 'It's a pity you're not sixteen.'

'Why?'

'You can't even look sixteen.'

We went another street-length before he spoke again. 'Eighteen I think it is anyway. I always get it mixed up with the age of consent.'

I still didn't understand.

'That's what's wrong with this bloody country,' he said. 'The lack of privacy. There's no way that a man can talk quietly to a boy under age. It's too cold for the park, and Liza wouldn't forgive me if you caught a chill. You are not allowed in a pub. Tea shops aren't open – not for any refreshment which a man can drink. I can go into a bar, but you aren't permitted. You can have a cup of tea in a tea shop, but too much tea – but don't tell Liza that – upsets me and they won't serve me what *I* want. So we'll just have to go on walking. It's different in France.'

'We could go home,' I suggested. I had begun to use the word 'home' consciously for the first time – I had never thought of my aunt's flat as home.

'But it's Liza I want to talk about. I can't talk in front of her.' He dropped into silence again for a couple of streets. Then he demanded, 'You are carrying those éclairs carefully, aren't you? Don't squeeze the bag. They are like toothpaste tubes if you squeeze them.'

I assured him that I was not squeezing them.

'She's very fond of éclairs,' he told me, 'and I wouldn't want them ruined.'

We walked perhaps a hundred yards further before he spoke again. 'I want you to tell her,' he said, 'tell her – but very gently, mind – that I won't be around for a month or two.'

'Why don't you come and tell her yourself?'

'I don't want to go into explanations. I don't like telling lies to Liza and the truth would only worry her. But tell her – tell her on my word of honour – on my word of honour, mind you say that – I'll be back, and everything will be hunky-dory. Just a few months away. That's all. And give her my love of course – don't forget that – my love.'

He stopped and asked in a tone of anxiety, 'You know where you are? You know the way back?'

'Yes,' I said, 'the butcher is at the next corner but one. I've been there often.'

'Well, son, I'll say goodbye then. Time for me to be off.' Yet he seemed strangely unwilling to go. He asked me, 'You two getting on well together?'

'Oh yes,' I said, 'fine.'

'You call her Mum like I told you?'

'She wants me to call her Liza.'

'Oh, that's Liza all over. She always likes things straight and true. I admire her for it, but the trouble is that straight and true can be a bit dangerous at times. For instance it's much safer if you called her Mum, not Liza.

If people hear you calling her Mum they sort of accept the situation. They don't ask questions.'

'She says it might make them wonder where I've sprung from.'

He pondered a little over my reply and then he said, 'Yes. I hadn't thought of that. Perhaps she's right. She does think things through. She learnt that in the school of suffering, poor Liza did. That devil your father . . .'

'Does she know my father?' I asked with curiosity, for I could hardly remember much of him myself.

'She knew him once, but don't you speak of him to her. I want her to forget.' He repeated 'to forget . . .' He added, 'And here I am forgetting the most important thing of all.' He took an envelope from his pocket and said, 'Give her that and tell her if there's any trouble, if she's short of anything . . . give it to she knows who.'

'To she knows who,' I repeated. It was a difficult message to memorize, like a phrase in a grammar lesson.

He asked, 'Is she happy with you there?'

'She seems all right,' I said.

'I don't want her to feel lonely – ever. Does she speak of me sometimes?'

'Oh yes,' I told him. 'She's always wondering when you'll turn up. She listens to footsteps.'

'I think,' he said with a kind of humble doubt, 'that she's a bit fond of me. In her own way of course.'

That tone of his came back to my mind when she said to me in her turn (I had just given her the envelope 'with his love'), 'I do think he likes me a lot – in his own way.' They neither of them seemed to be quite sure of the other's way. She added, 'You like him, don't you?'

We seemed, between the three of us in those days, to be doing a lot of thinking.

'You've got to get to know the Captain,' she repeated and she spoke in such an earnest tone that I can remember the exact phrase she used to this day. It was as if for a moment she had let me into the important secret which would help to explain what was already a mysterious past and any future, equally mysterious, which was likely to come.

(4)

As for the immediate future – well, perhaps not really the immediate, for I cannot remember now what length of time passed before we saw the Captain again and I have no memory of his return. Was it after weeks or months? Never mind, my memory leaps ahead to an evening when he took me to a movie house in order to see a film – it was I think called *King Kong*. (It was by that time already an ancient film even to my young eyes, but I remember how the Captain remarked to me as he bought the tickets, 'In this old flea-house you can see all the old films, and the old films are always the best.') There were few people in the cinema, for it was very early evening, but he took great care about our seats – a little too close for my eyesight and I asked whether we couldn't go back a few rows. The answer was 'No', firmly stated, and I assumed that the Captain had become short-sighted with age, for a man in his forties was to me as old as the pyramids. King Kong, if it was King Kong, clambered about the skyscrapers with a blonde girl – whose name I don't remember – in his arms. Every man's hand was against him – police, soldiers, even firemen I seem to remember. The girl kicked a bit, but she soon became quiescent.

'It's a great story,' the Captain whispered into my right ear.

'Yes.'

I believe that in the story the authorities – whoever they were – even brought planes into action against King Kong, who naturally interested me much more than the burden he carried.

'Why doesn't he drop her?' I asked.

I suppose I sounded very heartless to the Captain, for he replied harshly, 'He loves her, boy. Can't you understand that – he loves her?' But of course I couldn't understand. I had watched her kicking King Kong and to me love was more or less the same thing as liking, except that it might involve kissing, and kissing to me had little importance. Kissing had been something imposed on me by my aunt, but surely all the same neither liking nor loving could involve kicking. One kicked an enemy, in order to hurt. I realized that well enough, although I had never desired to hurt anyone except a boy called Twining who had made my life miserable as an Amalekite at a period which now began to seem years away.

An odd thing came to my notice when the lights went on. I saw that the Captain had tears in his eyes. I felt sorry for King Kong, but not to that extent. After all he was the stronger and he could have kicked back – as I couldn't with Twining who was two years older. I assumed that it was something else which had disturbed the Captain and I asked him, 'Is anything the matter?'

'The poor chap,' he said, 'all the world was against him.'

'I liked King Kong, but why did he carry the girl around all that time when she didn't like him?'

'How do you know she didn't like him?'

'Because she kicked him.'

'A kick or two doesn't mean anything. It's a woman's way. He loved her. You can be sure of that.'

That meaningless word 'love' again. How often my aunt had asked me, 'Do you love me?' And of course I had always answered 'Yes.' It was the easiest way out of a difficult situation. I couldn't very well reply, 'You bore the pants off me.' She was a good woman in her way, but now I couldn't help comparing her sandwiches with the meal which the Captain had given me at The Swan. I knew already that I liked the Captain, and that soft word 'love' with its mysterious demands would never come between us, I felt sure.

We walked a little way together from the cinema and at a street corner he paused and asked me as he had once before, 'You know the way home?' The word 'home' still made me hesitate a little, even though I had begun to use it experimentally myself. It was the word which my aunt had always used and on those brief occasions when I had seen the Devil he would of course use it too, saying 'Time to go home, boy,' though all he meant was the train to Richmond and my aunt's house. I said, 'Home?'

'To Liza,' he said, and I had the feeling that somehow I had failed him, but I didn't know how.

'Of course,' I said, 'it's only three streets away. Aren't you coming?'

'Better not.' He put a newspaper into my hands and

said, 'Give her this. Tell her to read page two, but not to worry. Everything's going to be OK.'

So I went on to the place they so wanted me to call home, though I was a little disappointed that he was not coming with me.

3

To love and to like – it must have been difficult for me as a child to learn how to distinguish between the two. Even in later years, when sexual desire began to play its part, I would find myself wondering, do I love this girl or do I really only like her because of the pleasure that for the time being we share?

As I went back home, carrying the newspaper, I was pretty certain that I liked the Captain, but I wasn't at all certain yet whether I liked Liza. Both of them were mysterious to me, but while I found the mystery of the Captain interesting, the mystery of Liza was like a disappointment; there was a sense of something lacking between us.

I gave her the newspaper and the message, but she put the newspaper away in a drawer in the kitchen and I knew that she wasn't going to read it so long as I remained there.

'What's on page two?' I asked her boldly.

'What do you mean page two?'

'The newspaper. He said you had to read page two.'

'Oh, it's only one of his jokes,' she said and she began to lay the table for our supper.

That night I couldn't sleep and when all was quiet I went down on tiptoe to the kitchen. I found the paper still there in the waste-paper basket, and I carried it up to my sofa bed.

All the same I didn't at once turn to the page the Captain had named. I was too excited. I felt as though I were on the brink of learning something about the Captain of vital importance. He had admitted to me on our first day together that he didn't always tell the truth, but in my young eyes a newspaper invariably contained truth, gospel truth. How often in the past I had heard my aunt exclaim about some extraordinary, even inconceivable, event, like the birth of a hippo or a rhinoceros in the London zoo, 'Of course it's true. It's in the papers.'

I can still see the front page of the *Telegraph* – the Captain was a *Telegraph* man (the *Telegraph*, I can believe now, went with the bowler hat, the walking-stick and the trimmed moustache – it was a stage property to help him create a character). A headline blazed up at me in big type conveying some totally uninteresting news – perhaps the fall of a government – I can't pretend to remember now. If only it had been murder . . . but it wasn't any story worth sticking in a twelve-year-old mind. But two stories on page two remain with me to this day: one was of a suicide of a rather horrible kind – a man who drenched himself in petrol and then set light to himself with a match, and the other dealt with what was called a gang robbery. Gangs were a feature of my imagination: the Amalekites were a gang. Apparently this gang had tied up and gagged a jeweller in a district called Wimbledon. He had been working late, 'taking stock', when a man of 'military bearing' had knocked on the door and asked the way to Baxter Street – a street unknown in Wimbledon. After the man had turned away and before the jeweller had time to close his door the gang had arrived, and with them when they left went the whole

(48)

stock, valued at several thousand pounds. There was no evidence that the man with 'the military bearing' was concerned in the robbery and the police appealed to him to come forward and help in their inquiries. It was believed that the same gang had been concerned in another robbery some weeks before.

I crept down and replaced the paper, and afterwards, lying on the sofa with sleep a long way off, I wondered at the strange coincidence that the street which was said not to exist bore my own name. My adopted mother next day seemed harassed and apprehensive. I had an impression that she was in fear of a strange caller. Twice there was a ring at the bell and she sent me to answer it, while she waited at the bottom of the stairs with that anxious look on her face. The first time it proved to be only the milkman and the second time someone who had got the street number wrong. In the middle of supper that night — as usual, my favourite dish, a hamburger with an egg on top — she spoke up suddenly apropos of nothing at all, with a kind of ferocity as though she were contradicting a remark of mine (but I had been as silent as herself). 'He's a good man,' she said. 'He'd never do anything that was really wicked. It's not in his nature. You should know that.'

'Know what?'

'Sometimes I think he's just too kind to live. He makes me scared.'

It was during the prolonged absence of the Captain which followed that Liza began to worry about my education. 'You ought to be learning things,' she told me over a cup of tea.

'What things?'

'Pretty nearly everything,' she said. 'Like sums.'

'I was never much good at sums.'

'Spelling.'

'My spelling's not bad.'

'Geography. If only the Captain would return he'd teach you that. You see he's a very travelled man.'

'Is he travelling now?'

'I expect he is.'

'You don't think he might have set himself alight?' I asked, remembering page two.

'Good heavens no. What makes you say that?'

'It was in that *Telegraph* he sent you.'

'So you read that paper?'

'Yes.'

'And you said nothing. That wasn't straight of you. The Captain wants you to be straight. He says that one day you'll look after me when he's gone.'

'He's gone now.'

'He means gone away for ever.'

'You'd miss him badly, wouldn't you?'

'It would be like dying – only worse. I want to be the one that goes first. But he says I've got to look after you. I think that's why he brought you here. To make sure I don't go first.'

'Are you very sick?' I asked with the cold curiosity of my age.

'No, but I was once. That was the first time he saw me – he came with your father to the hospital. Sometimes when he looks at me – he looks at me in a scared sort of way. As though I were still lying sick in that bed . . . Then I get sore at him. I don't want him scared because of me. He might do something rash.'

This conversation was perhaps my second lesson in what love might mean between two grown-up people. Love, it was quite clear to me now, meant fear, and I suppose it was the same fear which made Liza go out very early each morning to buy a *Telegraph* so that she might know the worst – the dreaded sequel to whatever it was she had read on page two, but when she was back in the safety of the kitchen she didn't know where to look, she had to turn every page, even the sports and financial pages, and she no longer hid from me that she was seeking some sort of news of the Captain with a deadly apprehension.

I cannot pretend that all these details which I am trying so hard to reconstruct from my memory are necessarily true, but I feel myself today driven by a compulsive passion now that we are separated to make these two people live before my eyes again, to bring them back out of the shadows and set them to play their sad parts as closely as possible to the truth. I am only too well aware of how I may be weaving fact into fiction but without any intention of betraying the truth. I want above anything else to make the two of them clear to myself, so that they will continue to live as visibly as two photographs might seem to do propped up on a shelf beside my bed, but I don't own a single photograph of either of them. Why am I so possessed by them? Of the Captain I have heard nothing for years, and Liza, whom I left of my own accord, I see only from time to time, always with a sense of guilt. It's not because of any love I feel for them. It is as though I had taken them quite coldbloodedly as fictional characters to satisfy this passionate desire of mine to write.

4

The bell rang, but only once – and that wasn't the right signal for the Captain.

'Shall I go?' I asked. 'Perhaps it's the postman.'

'He came when you were out fetching a paper. Don't go. It may be one of the neighbours.'

The bell rang a second time.

'They can see the light in the basement,' I told her.

'The inquisitive bitches,' Liza said. 'That Mrs Lowndes at twenty-three asked me who you were. I was out cleaning the steps. I said you were my son and that you'd been living with your father until he died. Do you know what she said? "Why is he not at school?" she said.'

The bell rang a third time more imperiously.

'What did you tell her?' I asked.

'I said, "He has private lessons," but I don't think she believed me.'

The bell rang again twice. 'Suppose it's the police,' Liza said.

'What would they want?'

'You'd better go and see. Be careful. If they ask about the Captain, you don't know him, you've never seen him, and he's not here.'

I went slowly and nervously up from the basement and gave the bell enough time to ring again. Then I bent down and looked through the keyhole, but I could see only a section of grey overcoat slashed open by a pocket. I opened the door and there was my father.

'The Devil,' I exclaimed before I could stop myself.

My father was a white-bearded burly man with a fine set of teeth for his age, but perhaps they were capped. They flashed their double row at me now in quite a genial fashion. 'May the Devil come in?' he asked, and I stood aside for him.

'Liza,' he called, 'Liza,' looking up the stairs.

'She's in the basement,' I told him, and he picked his way down carefully step by step, for the stairs were narrow and his feet were big.

'So it's you,' Liza said. She stood by the kitchen table with a carving-knife in her hand, but that was only because she had been in the middle of washing up. 'How did you know?'

'I got a picture postcard from Roger.'

'Roger?'

'It was a picture of Bruges cathedral. He asked me to look you both up in case you needed help because he'd been away a long time.'

'Who's Roger?' I asked.

'Oh, I forgot. He likes to call himself the Captain, doesn't he?' He turned on me. 'You've been causing quite a bit of trouble, Victor.'

The name angered me. I said, 'I'm Jim now.'

'Well, it's your mother who chose Victor. I never liked the name. It sounded a bit like boasting. I think it was because you were born on May something or other when we celebrate the day the Germans surrendered.'

'I wasn't. I was born in September.'

'Oh, then there must have been another reason. Perhaps she thought to have you at all was *her* victory. Over me. I wasn't so keen on a child.'

'Well, I'm Jim now.'

'Jim's a shade better, but it's still a bit on the common side.'

'We don't need any help from you,' Liza said.

'I wish that silly fellow had told me earlier where you were both hiding. It would have saved me a lot of bother about Victor. Oh, all right, Jim, if you like it better. There was first your aunt, and then a fool called Bates. He wrote me an extraordinary letter. Said he was your headmaster. Never heard of him till then. I always paid the bills to a man they called the bursar. But your aunt was the worst of the lot. How are you, old girl?'

'I'm all right.'

'No more trouble with your insides?'

'No.'

'What's happening with Roger – I mean the Captain?'

'He's looking after us. You don't need to worry. I tell you he's looking after us fine.'

'From Bruges?'

'Work takes him away now and then.'

'Work? The Captain? Don't make me laugh.' He looked all around him at the kitchen. 'You won't offer me a cup of tea, Liza, for old time's sake?'

'Sit down then if you must.'

I could see that he wasn't in the least daunted by her reluctance. 'I suppose he's in trouble again.'

'You might as well take off your coat if you are going to have a cup of tea.'

'No, no. I won't stay long. I'm only a bird of passage,

Liza. But your Captain went a bit far when he kidnapped the boy. No wonder he's hiding in Bruges.'

'He isn't hiding in Bruges. And he didn't kidnap him. He won him off you. Fair and square at backgammon. You can't cheat at backgammon.'

'There's never been a game invented yet at which you can't find a way to cheat. Anyway it was chess we played not backgammon. It's difficult to cheat at backgammon, but chess – especially after a drink or two. One of you gets a bit tired. The attention wanders. You switch a piece and, lo and behold, checkmate it is. Roger, you know, has a way of getting his details a little wrong. Even that name Captain which you call him. He was a sergeant not a captain when the Germans were supposed to have nabbed him, and I doubt if they promoted him to an officer in captivity. If he ever was in captivity – that sort of captivity. He has a lot of imagination.'

'I don't believe you. You were always jealous of him.'

'It doesn't really matter anyway, does it? If he wants to be a captain . . . though it *was* a bit dangerous nabbing the boy.'

'He didn't nab him. You know very well – he won him at backgammon.'

'I told you it was chess we played and he didn't even win at that without cheating.'

'You wrote a letter for him to the headmaster, saying he could take him away.'

'Yes, for an afternoon – to give him lunch and a movie. Oh well, we won't quarrel about little details like that, Liza. But what on earth made him do it?'

'He didn't want me to be lonely, that's why. He thinks of others.'

'Perhaps you are right. It's a real shame you couldn't have a child of your own.'

'And that's your fault.'

'You know well enough you didn't want the one you lost, Liza. Blame that clumsy doctor, not me.'

'I didn't want any child *you* had fathered – that's true enough.'

Their argument was quite beyond me in those days and it remained a mystery for many years, so that it was an argument meaningless to me then which I am trying to reproduce, and what I am writing now has to be based on my later knowledge. At that moment all that worried me was Liza's suppressed anger. I could see that she was hurt and that it was the Devil who had hurt her. There was no doubt at all in my mind which of them was to blame. 'Why don't you go?' I said to the Devil, and putting into my voice all the courage I possessed I added, 'You are not wanted here.'

'Look who's talking. I'm your father, boy.'

'And she's my mother,' I said, getting the word out with a sense of confidence and triumph for the first time.

'Bravo,' the Devil said, 'bravo.'

'There's your tea. Drink it,' Liza told him.

'If I could have another lump of sugar. You've forgotten, Liza, that I have a very sweet tooth.'

'I don't want to remember anything about you. There's the sugar basin. Take as much as you want.'

'Perhaps you ought to forget the Captain too, if you want to forget me. After all you wouldn't have met him without me.'

'That's true and I'll say thank you for that, but for nothing else in the world.'

'Oh come. I wasn't as bad to you as all that, was I?'

'You made me have a dead child, and he's given me Jim.'

'I only hope you'll be able to keep your Jim.'

'Oh, I don't need any money from you. The Captain . . .'

'I wasn't meaning money, Liza, but I warn you that his aunt's on the track. She's even talking of a private detective.'

'And I suppose you'll tell her where we are?'

'Do you really think I'm all that of a devil, Liza? No, I promise you I'll tell his aunt nothing, nothing. She reminds me too much of my wife – but the sister's much worse. I'm sure you'll look after the boy a lot better than she's ever done.'

He finished his tea and stared into his cup as though he were telling a fortune. He said, 'You won't believe me, Liza, but I'd like to help.'

'I don't believe you.'

'And yet you believe *him*.'

'I've good reason to.'

'Oh he's been telling you a lot of stories. I used to believe them myself. He's not what I'd call a very truthful man. Even his moustache . . . What colour does he fancy now?'

5

(1)

But his moustache had quite gone some weeks later, after I had run upstairs and opened the door because the bell had sounded the correct, the safe and the longed-for code. I think perhaps a kind of affection for each other had grown a little in both of us during the Captain's absence. I was beginning to be quite fond of Liza, but it was still with the easily transferable affection of a child, and her affection may well have been an almost automatic response to my own and could have been cut off just as readily. But it was the Captain who occupied our thoughts and our conversation. 'The Captain always says . . .' 'You know the Captain told me once that when he was a prisoner . . .'

And yet it was not the same Captain that we had known who stood waiting outside the door. A Captain he might still be, but a tall bearded sea captain with no stick across his shoulder like a rifle, but a stick carried in his fist like a weapon against pirates. I gaped at him and didn't move for a moment to let him in, and behind him beside the pavement was a car. A car!

'Is that yours?' I asked him.

'Of course it's mine,' he snapped at me. 'Where's Liza? Is Liza all right?'

He pushed me aside and went down the stairs two at a time. I saw them greet each other. She had taken a pace or two to meet him, but they halted a foot apart. They didn't kiss: they didn't even touch. It was as though they were frightened of each other after the months of absence. She said, 'You've grown a beard.'

'Yes.'

'Why?'

'It seemed a bit wiser.' He put his hand on her shoulder. 'You're all right, Liza?'

'I'm all right, but you . . .'

'Nothing to worry about.'

They kissed each other at last – not the kind of passionate kiss which I had seen only once on the screen at *King Kong* and remembered ever after, but a small timorous kiss on either cheek, as though even that gesture was something which could be dangerous to the loved one, like an infection. I turned away to close and lock the door with a second look at the car and a sense of disappointment, and when I joined them in the kitchen she was busy making the inevitable pot of tea, which I knew now that he only drank to please her.

'So the old Devil turned up,' the Captain remarked.

'He sat where you are sitting now.'

The Captain shifted uneasily back and forth on the hard chair as if he could still feel the warmth left there by my father's body and resented it.

'What did he have to say?'

'He said he wanted to help me.'

'And what did you tell him?'

'I said I didn't need any help from him.'

The Captain continued to shift uneasily in his chair. 'Perhaps that wasn't wise, Liza.'

'I don't *want* his help.'

'And I don't suppose he trusts *me* either.'

'Oh, that's for sure he doesn't.'

'A bit of regular money for you all the same – even from him – it would save you a lot of anxiety. I can't always be around.'

'We've managed all right so far.'

I don't pretend that I can remember correctly the details of this conversation. There are certain words which I do remember, but I invent far more of them, in order to fill in the gaps between their words, because I want so much to hear in my ears again the tone of their two voices. Above all I want to understand the only two people in whom I could recognize what I suppose can be described as a kind of love, a kind which to this day I have certainly never felt in myself. Of one thing I am almost sure at least, that I heard him, after a long pause, ask her, 'Did he make you unhappy again?' and her quick reply, 'He can't. Not any longer.'

Did the Captain stay with us that night? By the nature of things I would never have known that – they were far too discreet. When I went to bed I tried to keep awake as long as I could hear voices below, to reassure me that I wasn't alone. I listened too for the sound of a car going away, but I went to sleep before the voices had ceased. I only know that next morning he was there at breakfast and I remember that detail because for the first time the question of my schooling was raised.

I think it came about because I asked him the moment that I joined them about his car. 'It's really yours?'

'Of course it's mine.'

'What kind is it?'

'A Morris Minor.'

'Is that a good car?'

'It's not a Rolls. It's good enough as things are.'

'Will you teach me to drive it?'

'No. At your age it's against the law. And talking about the law,' he added to Liza, 'I think there are laws about schooling, but I'm damned if I know what they are. Jim can read and he can write – whatever else does a boy need? The rest just comes with living. Anyway there are things which I can teach him better than any school-master.'

'Science?'

'Oh, I don't know very much about science. But I can't see Jim ever being a scientist.'

'Religion?'

'That's more of a woman's job. Your job.'

'I don't know a lot about religion either.'

'Give him a Bible and let him read it for himself. You can't force religion on a boy, Liza. One learns it as one goes along or one doesn't.'

'You never did, I suppose.'

'Then you suppose too much. I've told you before that, when I walked down off the Pyrenees after I escaped, I found a monastery. They didn't ask for any papers, they didn't go to the police – what I saw going on was all a lot of nonsense, of course, but they were good men, at least they were good to me. When you are not a good man yourself you respect a good man. I would prefer to die with a good man around. A good man teaches a lot of nonsense and a bad man teaches truth, but what the hell is the difference when you come to die? I'm not the one to teach the boy nonsense. Let him read the Bible and learn to judge it for himself. I'll teach him geography.'

'And then there's always languages. I wouldn't want a

boy of mine to be more ignorant than others.'

'Good for you, Liza. You've said it.'

'Said what?'

'You've never said it before. "A boy of mine."'

'Well, in a sort of way I suppose he is now . . .'

'As for languages – no problem there, Liza. You can buy him gramophone records – German Self-Taught, Spanish . . . And as it happens I've got a smattering of both – and you know why. I can sort of help him along the path . . .'

So it was that I happily escaped school for the time being and began with what one might call a private education. The lessons were not very regular: they depended on the availability of the Captain who was very often absent. They were in a way secretive – which made them more enjoyable, for the neighbours would see me going off at the right time for school and they never saw my quick and furtive return for the lessons held in my room. Otherwise rumours would have certainly reached the authorities. So without exactly knowing it I was, in my small way, already following in the Captain's illegal tracks.

I remember little of the language classes; I have only an impression that the Captain was a good deal more at ease in German than he was in Spanish, perhaps because, if what he told me was true, he had spent far more time as a prisoner in Germany than as an escaped prisoner in Spain. This too affected his geography lessons. They were lessons drawn from the experience of a traveller in rather unusual circumstances and perhaps they were more vivid than the superficial second-hand knowledge of a school teacher.

I will try to reproduce part of a typical lesson in geography.

'If you want to go from Germany to Spain, how would you go?' he asked me.

'I'd take a plane,' I said.

'No, no, that's against the rules. We are playing a sort of game. Like Monopoly. There's a war on, so in this game you've got to go on foot.'

'Why not in a car?'

'You haven't got a car.'

I was still puzzled by his own car. Had he paid for it and how had he got the money or was it like that smoked salmon lunch?

He had bought a school atlas and he laid it open before me, and I think he was relieved to find that I could read a map reasonably well with all the symbols and colours which indicate rivers, railways, mountains.

'I suppose I'd walk into France,' I said.

'Oh no, you wouldn't. France is under enemy occupation. There are Germans everywhere.'

I tried again. 'Belgium?' I suggested.

'That's better. There are Germans there too, but you've been given an address, see. A safe house. A bit like this basement here. In a town called Liège. Find Liège.'

He spelt the name out for me and I found it, but I still felt a bit at sea. 'Why do I want to go to Spain?'

'Because it's neutral, and then you can get to Portugal and so to England. Where's Portugal?'

After a little search I found Portugal. 'Portugal's on our side,' he explained, 'but you have to reach Spain first. How do you do that?'

Now that I knew geography was a kind of war game I began really to enjoy it. I looked closely at the map.

'I'd have to go through France somehow in spite of the Germans.'

'That's right. You find in the safe house that there are four Air Force officers in hiding like you and there's a brave young woman – no older than Liza – and she's going with you. All the way to the Pyrenees by train. The Pyrenees are mountains. Find them.'

This took longer, for I got mixed up with the Ardennes on the way.

'But why don't the Germans stop us?'

'She's got false papers for all of you. The others can talk a bit of French. Better than the Germans can anyway. You can't, so she binds up your jaw with a bandage, blood-stained, so that you can't speak. A bomb casualty, she tells everyone, and she's in charge of you. As for the others she says that she just happened to meet them on the train, and they'd made friends. You get through Paris safely and you change trains. You get out finally at a place called Tarbes.' He spelt the name out. 'Now find Tarbes.'

It was only a game we were playing and I didn't take it as a piece of history. How much of the Captain's story was true I don't know to this day, but I certainly enjoyed our lessons in geography, especially when I passed over the Pyrenees by night, barefoot in the snow, listening for the sucking noise made by the boots of the German patrols. All the later geography lessons have faded from my memory, so that even today I can't visualize Spain and Portugal with the same clarity as West Germany, Belgium and France, but in Spain the geography lesson would sometimes merge into history.

The Captain had a special sympathy for Drake and Sir

Henry Morgan. 'They were pirates,' he said, 'sailing the Seven Seas in search of gold.'

'What did they do with it?'

'They seized it from the Spaniards.'

He spoke of the Spanish mule trains which carried the gold from the Pacific side of Panama to the Atlantic (he marked the route on the map) and how Drake ambushed them on the way.

'They were thieves?'

'No, I told you. They were pirates.'

'What did the Spaniards do?'

'They fought hard. They were real sportsmen.'

'People got killed?'

'People get killed in boxing too.' He was silent for quite a while, thinking his own thoughts. Then he said, 'Thieves steal trash. Pirates steal millions.' Again there was a prolonged moment of reflection. 'I suppose you might say that thieves could be called pirates too, but in a very small way of business. They haven't had the luck and opportunity which the pirates had.'

This particular lesson would be broken by a lot of silences, and a few geographical names. When I tried to get him moving too rapidly into Portugal I failed. He said, after one silence, 'If I had the money I'd like to go where Drake went – Panama and all the countries over there where the gold came from, but Liza wouldn't be happy – she wouldn't feel at home. All the same one day perhaps . . .' I put my finger on the map and said for the second time, 'But Portugal. What's Portugal like?'

'An agglomeration of sardines.' He used a word which I doubt if either of us really understood. 'Forget Portugal. Did they teach you poetry at school, boy?'

I began to recite a piece which at school I had been made to learn by heart. I have forgotten it now, but it was about brave Horatius keeping some bridge or other. He interrupted me, 'Give me King Kong any day of the week.' He added apologetically, 'I'm not one for poetry as a rule – but there's a bit of verse which sticks in my head by a fellow called Kipling. Oh, they wouldn't have understood him at your school. "Brave Horatius",' he repeated with scorn. 'What a name for a man. Kipling wrote what a man feels, anyway a man like me. He sort of speaks to me. Perhaps if only Liza felt the same way we might have been out of here long ago and we'd be rich and snug and safe.'

'Aren't you safe here?' I asked.

He didn't answer my question – at least not directly.

> 'God bless the something islands,' he said,
>   'Where never warrants come,
> God bless the just Republics,
>   That give a man a home.'

'That's poetry?' I asked.

'That's poetry, real poetry, Jim. It speaks to you. They can stuff your brave Horatius. Do you know what I dream of?'

I don't know why but I answered, 'Tortoises?'

'Tortoises! I don't dream of tortoises. Why on earth should I dream of tortoises? When I dream it's when I'm awake, not when I'm asleep. I dream of all that gold which Drake took from the mules in Panama. I dream that we are rich all three of us, rich and safe, and I dream that Liza is able to buy anything that takes her fancy.'

'Does she dream it too?'

'I know very well she doesn't, and I don't think she likes me to dream it either.'

I am doing my best to describe a typical lesson which I received from the Captain, but I realize only too well that my description cannot be factually accurate. It has passed through the memory and the memory rejects and alters, much as the Captain may have changed a lot of facts when he recounted his wartime experiences. Sometimes Liza sat with us during a lesson, and I noticed then that her favourite story — of his escape to Spain — which even found a place in his language lessons as well as his geography ones (on one occasion at least he even attempted a bit of modern history) — became more detailed when she was with us, and the details did not always tally; it was as though with Liza in his audience he wanted to make the story a bit more interesting. Perhaps, I sometimes thought, he may deliberately lie a little. For example when he described to me his escape with his companions across the Pyrenees he told me — that I'm sure — how they lay in the dark listening to the noise of the boots made by the German patrol, but later when Liza was sitting with us he added a dramatic detail, telling how a stone was dislodged and fell from above and struck his ankle and to this day in damp weather the pain came back and he would find himself limping, something which I had never seen him do.

(2)

The beard did not last more than a week or two. One morning when I came down to breakfast I found the

Captain was busy shaving it off. Perhaps because he was whistling at the same time he cut himself twice. 'I never feel at home in this thing,' he told me. 'It always reminds me of those fuliginous days in the Pyrenees. No chance of shaving there. Anyway Liza doesn't like it. She says she gets prickled.'

He turned around, razor in hand, to where Liza was making the tea and exhibited himself. 'That's the way you like it, Liza?'

'I don't like to see you bleeding.'

'A little blood-letting does no one any harm.' That was a phrase that I'm quite sure he used, for it remained in my head for years, though I have no idea why. They were also the last words I can remember him saying for some weeks, for he didn't come in that day for supper, and the next morning he wasn't there for breakfast.

'Where's the Captain?' I asked.

'How would I know?' Liza said in a tone which, when I think of it now, comes back to me as almost a cry of despair.

'But he said we were going to have another history lesson,' I complained with the egotistic disappointment of my age, and, just as I feared, it was a religious lesson from Liza which took its place.

The religious lessons had been much less of a success with me. Of course at school with the Amalekites I had attended what my fellows called 'Divvers', but I was a bit vague about the events in the New Testament except for the birth at the inn (not the sort of inn I felt sure which served gin and tonics), the crucifixion and the resurrection. All these had impressed me like a fairy story with an unlikely happy ending. (I never really believed that Cinderella would marry the Prince.)

Liza had obeyed the Captain's instruction and bought me a Bible at a second-hand bookshop, and I dipped into it now and then, but I found the old-fashioned language very difficult and the business of the Virgin birth confused me. One evening before she turned off the light over my sofa I asked Liza to explain it. 'I always thought a virgin meant . . .' But she interrupted me quickly and left me in darkness. I thought that perhaps she didn't like talking about babies because she hadn't succeeded in having one of her own and the word 'virgin' obviously embarrassed her too.

All the same – to please the Captain – she would ask me every Sunday to read a bit of the Bible out loud to her, but I soon discovered a way of escaping this routine by twice choosing passages which she couldn't possibly explain. For this I dived into that part which was called the Old Testament and this except for the history of the Amalekites had played a very small part in Divvers.

I asked her first if the Bible was a holy book, and she said, 'Of course it is.' So I read her this: 'And thou, Son of Man, take thee a sharp knife, take thee a barber's razor, and cause it to pass upon thy head and upon thy beard: then take the balances to weigh and divide the hair. Thou shalt burn with fire a third part in the midst of the city, and thou shalt take a third part and smite about it with a knife, and a third part thou shalt scatter in the wind. Thou shalt also take thereof a few in number and bind them in their skirts.'

I asked, 'Do you think the Captain was doing all that

when he cut himself shaving? Whose skirts . . . ?' But Liza was gone before I could finish my sentence.

The second time of reading aloud I had come on a really good passage. I said, 'This is difficult. There are words I don't understand. Will you help me?' And I began to read.

'And the Babylonians came to her in the bed of love, and they defiled her with their whoredom, and she was polluted with some. So she discovered her whoredoms and discovered her nakedness. Yet she multiplied her whoredoms, in calling to remembrance the days of her youth, wherein she had played the harlot in the land of Egypt.' I probably mispronounced 'whoredoms', but anyway Liza left without explaining the words and she never asked me to read aloud again.

(3)

This time the Captain when he returned was again wearing a moustache, though in a different style and colour to the one I had known. It was in the late dusk when the code rang and we hardly had enough time to greet him before the bell began to ring again – imperiously. I had grown accustomed to think of any bell which rang as a form of code, and this one had a kind of familiarity, but one thing was certain: it couldn't be the Captain for there he stood in the kitchen holding his breath as he listened. I had a good memory and at the third ring I felt pretty sure that its imperious sound indicated that my father stood outside.

'I'm not sure,' I said, 'but I think it's the Devil.'

'Don't open the door,' Liza said.

'No, let the bastard in,' the Captain said. 'We are not afraid of him.'

I was right. It was my father, and he was not alone. What was far worse, my aunt was with him.

'So there you are,' my aunt rapped out, 'Victor,' and I suppose I must have flinched at the hated and almost forgotten name.

I think my father noticed my fear. 'I'm sorry, Jim,' he said, and I gave him credit for remembering this time my change of name, 'I had to bring her, for she'd have come anyway without me.'

'Who's this woman?' my aunt demanded.

I had gained a little courage from my father. 'Liza's my mother,' I said with defiance.

'You are insulting the dear dead and departed.' My aunt had always the strange habit on certain occasions of talking like the Book of Common Prayer. I suppose that it came from all her church going.

'I do think,' the Devil said, 'that we should all sit down and discuss matters in a quiet and civilized way.'

'Who's that man and what's he doing here?'

'Haven't you eyes?' Liza spoke up at last. 'He's having a cup of tea. Is there anything wrong in that?'

'What's his name?'

'The Captain,' I said.

'That's not a name.'

'It would really be much better, Muriel, if you sat down,' my father said, and the Captain pulled up a chair and my aunt sat on the edge of it as though she feared her bottom might be infected by whichever of us had sat in it last.

'She's been employing a private detective,' my father

told us. 'I don't know how he got on the track. They are damned clever some of those fellows, and of course your neighbours probably talk.'

'I know which one,' Liza said.

'She asked me to come with her. She said she was afraid of violence.'

'Afraid?' the Captain asked. 'That one afraid?'

'Kidnappers,' my aunt spat out.

'Now, now,' the Devil said, 'you are not at all just, Muriel. I told you it was a fair game and that he won.'

'You told me he cheated.'

'Of course he cheated, Muriel. So did I. Women,' he appealed to the Captain, 'don't understand the point of a game like chess. Anyway I've explained to her that legally I have custody of the boy and that I've given my permission to Liza . . .'

'My sister asked me on her deathbed to look after . . .'

'Oh yes, and I consented at the time, but that's a long while ago. You said yourself last year that you were tired of the responsibility.'

'I was not too tired to do my duty. It's time you did your duty too.' She turned on Liza. 'The boy's not receiving any education. There are laws about that.'

'You certainly have a good detective, Miriam,' the Devil said.

'Muriel! You ought to know my name after all these years.'

'Sorry, Muriel. Muriel and Miriam always sound so much alike to me.'

'I don't see the likeness.'

'Jim's having lessons at home,' Liza said.

'You'll have to satisfy the local education authority.'

'What would he know about it?'

'He'll know all there is to know after I've seen him. Who's teaching Victor?'

'I am,' the Captain said. 'I'm teaching him geography and history. I leave religion to Liza. He's already learned to add, subtract and multiply. It's all anyone needs. I don't suppose you know much algebra yourself.'

'What are your qualifications, Mr . . . Mr . . . ?'

'Call me Captain, ma'am. Everyone else does.'

'What's the capital of Italy, Victor?'

'Modern geography doesn't deal with names, ma'am. All that's old hat. Geography deals with landscapes. Geography teaches you how to travel about the world. You tell her, Jim, how to get from Germany to Spain.'

'I go to Belgium first, then Liège. I take a train there to Paris, and from Paris I take another train to Tarbes.'

'Where on earth is Tarbes?'

'There, you see, ma'am. You don't know names either, but Jim, he knows how to go from Tarbes. Go on, Jim.'

'After Tarbes I'd walk across the Pyrenees. By night.'

'It's a lot of nonsense. What do you mean "walk across by night"?'

'Listening for the sound of German boots squish-squashing in the snow.'

That sentence, I suspect, was the end of my private education. A few weeks later I found myself at a local school. I wasn't unhappy there, for I wasn't an Amalekite. I felt a sense of freedom as I walked through the London streets alone, as though, like the men who passed by me, I was on my way to an office and a job. The lessons were not as interesting as the Captain's had been, but I had already learnt that I could not trust the Captain for any regular lessons even in geography.

6

I think it was two years or more after I started school that the longest separation we had known came about. It was a Saturday afternoon and I was free from school. Liza was out buying bread and for once she had left me alone with my lesson books. Then the bell rang. It wasn't the Captain's code, nor was it my father's. This was a ring, quiet, reassuring, even friendly. The ringer waited what seemed to be a polite time before he rang again, and the ring still remained unurgent, undemanding. I knew that Liza would never have opened the door willingly to any ring but the Captain's, but I was in charge now.

I called through the door, 'Who's there?' And a voice answered, 'Please open the door. I'm a police officer.' I felt excited and proud at my first social contact with a force which I had sometimes dreamed of one day joining, so I let him in.

He didn't look like a police officer; he wasn't in uniform and I was a little disappointed at that. Indeed in an odd way he reminded me of the Captain. Both wore ordinary clothes like a disguise, and I wondered if perhaps this might not be an unknown brother turning up. He said, 'I wanted to speak to your father.'

'He doesn't live here,' I told him without lying, because of course I thought that he meant the Devil.

'Where's your mother?'

'She's out buying bread.'

'I think I had better stay until she returns.'

He sat down in the one easy chair and looked more than ever like a relative on a visit. 'You a truthful boy?' he asked.

I thought it best to be accurate as I was speaking to one of the police. 'Sometimes,' I said.

'Where does your father live when he's not here?'

'He's never here,' I said.

'Never?'

'Oh, he's been here once or twice.'

'Once or twice? When was that?'

'The last about two years ago.'

'Not much of a father then?'

'Liza and I don't like having him around.'

'Who's Liza?'

'My mother.' I remembered again that I was expected to be truthful. 'Well, sort of,' I added.

'What do you mean – sort of?'

'My mother's dead.'

He gave a sigh. 'Do you mean Liza's dead?'

'No, of course she isn't. I told you. She's at the baker's.'

'My God, you're a difficult child to understand. I wish your "sort of mother" would come back. I've got questions I want to ask her. If your father doesn't live here where does he live?'

'I think my aunt told me once it was a place called Newcastle, but my aunt – she lives in Richmond,' (I went on talking and giving him all the information I could in order to show my goodwill) 'and they don't get on all that well together. She calls him the Devil.'

'Perhaps about that,' he said, 'judging from what you say, she may not be far wrong,' and at the same moment the door above opened and I heard Liza's footsteps on the stairs.

Something made me call out, 'Liza, there's a policeman here.'

'I could have told her that myself,' he said.

Liza came belligerently in, holding a loaf of bread like a brick that she was prepared to launch. 'A policeman?'

He tried to reassure her. 'I just wanted to ask you a few questions, ma'am. It won't take a moment. I think you may be able to give us a little help.'

'I won't help a policeman and that's that.'

'We are trying to trace a gentleman who goes by the name of Colonel Claridge.'

'I don't know any Colonel Claridge. I don't mix with Colonels. I've never known a Colonel. Can you see a Colonel coming into a kitchen like this? Just look at the stove there. A Colonel wouldn't be seen dead with a stove like that.'

'Sometimes, ma'am, he goes by other names. Victor for instance.'

'I tell you I don't know any Colonels or any Victors. You'll get nothing out of me.'

I have always wondered what might have happened after that visit and what it was that had happened before to cause it. Several years were to pass before I saw the Captain again. His visits then were short and I was not always there. Sometimes when I returned from school I would notice only a half-empty teacup.

Did I miss him? I have no memory of any emotion unless it was the occasional wild desire for something interesting to happen. Had I grown to love the Captain, this putative father who was now as distant from me as my real parent? Did I love Liza who looked after me, gave me the right food, dispatched me at the correct hour to school and welcomed me back with an impatient kiss? Did I love anyone? Did I know what love was? Do I know it now years later or is love something which I have read about in books? The Captain returned of course, he always seemed eventually to return.

Now that I have left Liza and abandoned what I had learned to call home, I only know of his absences at second-hand when I visit Liza. Sometimes a year has gone by, sometimes two. I have never heard her complain. I always use the same code on the bell, for otherwise I am sure that she would never let me in. I think she hopes always that it is he and not I who rings. Only three times have my visits coincided with one of his and I was well aware that he thought I was still living in the house. 'Been out shopping?' he asked on one occasion in a friendly and uninterested way, and another time he inquired perfunctorily about my work as a journalist. 'Doesn't keep you out too late?' he asked. 'You know how Liza hates the dark.' Liza appealed to me on that occasion when he happened to be the first to leave. 'Don't you ever say you aren't living here now. I don't want him to worry about me. He has enough worries.'

Why had I gone off and left her? Perhaps I had become too impatient at the comedy which Liza played more and more frequently during the long absences of the Captain. I felt that she played it to protect him from reproach, and I only bore it as long as he seemed likely to return one day and settle with us. I wasn't used to motherhood. What I had known before was aunthood which I hated, and perhaps I had begun to regard Liza as a substitute aunt more than as a substitute mother. I could put up with her as long as the Captain was around. The Captain never attempted to play the father. He was an adventurer, he belonged to that world of Valparaiso which I had dreamt about as a child, and like most boys I responded, I suppose, to the attraction of mystery, uncertainty, the absence of monotony, the worst feature of family life.

I refuse to feel guilt at leaving her. I am sure that he sends her money, while he is away, and in a curious fashion I feel that they are growing old together without me, even though now he seldom seems to be there. I have always wondered if perhaps . . .

PART

II

7

(1)

'I have always wondered.' What was it that I 'always wondered', I ask myself as I read this account of our life together, an account which I had begun to write years before but had abandoned when I left home. I found no answer to my question in it.

I had heard of Liza's grave state in hospital from the police and so I came to what I still reluctantly called my home to do all the tiresome things which are required when one prepares for the death of a parent. There was no real next of kin to whom I could pass the disagreeable task. Liza had been nearly killed in a stupid road accident as she crossed the street from the baker's where it had always been my duty years before to fetch the bread. The police found a letter for me in her pocket, a letter in which she typically reminded me to get vaccinated against the coming flu, and her near death gave me a passing sense of guilt at having left her, for otherwise it would have been I who had gone to fetch the bread and the accident would never have happened.

At the hospital, speaking with difficulty, she told me to destroy a lot of letters which she didn't want strangers to read. 'Why I kept them I don't know,' she said. 'He always writes a lot of nonsense.' She added, 'Don't let the Captain know that I'm here.'

'But if he turns up . . .'

'He won't. In his last letter he spoke about next year or

the next . . .' She added, 'Be kind to him. He's always been kind to us.'

I brought up the forbidden word. 'Does he love you?'

'Oh, love. They are always saying God loves us. If that's love I'd rather have a bit of kindness.'

I was prepared for his letters, but I was taken a little by surprise when I came on this unfinished story – fiction, autobiography? – which I have written here. It lay under several piles of letters preserved by Liza, neatly stacked and tied with rubber bands, in the kitchen drawer which was otherwise devoted to napkins and queer useless objects known in far-off days as doilies.

I didn't even recognize at first my own handwriting, so legible had it been in the past. My handwriting now after the passage of years and all the hasty work involved in cheap journalism, reports of trivial occasions for a newspaper which I at heart despise, is almost unreadable.

There had been a period in my youth when I had nursed the vain ambition to become what I thought of as a 'real writer' and I suppose it was then that I began this fragment. Perhaps I had chosen the form because I knew so little of the outside world which could possibly have any interest for others. I must have left this draft – of what? – when I abruptly and shamefacedly abandoned my basement life, taking the opportunity during one of Liza's rare absences, and with me went a little of the money which I found in her bedroom – there was enough left, I told myself, to last her till the next instalment from the Captain arrived. He had never failed her yet, and I thought the small contribution I had extorted was fair enough. She would certainly have spent much more on me in the months that followed and now I was gone she would have the next draft all to herself to play with – not that she ever played with money.

Liza, it was evident, had read my manuscript (I was glad to find when I went through it that it contained no wounding criticism of her maternal care), for she had scrawled on the last page, in her not very literary hand, what might well have served as a conventional epitaph on the Captain's tombstone, or perhaps she intended it to be a final reply to all the police officers who had come and worried her with questions: 'All the same whatever you say about him the Captain was very good to both of us. He was' (the 'was' had been crossed out) 'he is a very good man.' Characteristically she made no use of that mysterious term 'love'; there remained for the tombstone only this defiant recognition of the Captain's virtue. Had physical love (I wondered if that was the meaning behind my question-mark?) ever existed between these two odd people whom as a child I had less than half known?

I felt it very strange to find myself all alone, in the shabby basement in that rundown street in Camden Town, reading a document which I had composed so many years before, and afterwards, one by one, I glanced through the hitherto unseen letters from the Captain, all of them preserved in their envelopes bearing foreign stamps. I soon discovered it was much against the Captain's will that he had continued to address them to the house in Camden Town. The Captain had at least been good to both of us in his intention. During all his absences he had written with some regularity, though seldom with an address more exact than a poste restante. The last disappearance of which I had been a witness occurred a short while before the visit of yet another plain-clothes officer. Afterwards a small parcel would arrive at intervals of two or three months, sometimes containing a letter, sometimes not, but always money or valuables. The parcel would be thrust through the letter-box by a strange hand which had first rung the coded signal on the bell.

'I don't like it. I can't bear it,' Liza once remarked to me. 'It's not fair. That was a secret between him and me. When it rings I think . . . perhaps this time . . . and it never is. Sometimes that code seems now the only thing we ever really shared.' She added dutifully, 'Except you of course.'

Then for months the money ceased to come, and no letter either. Luckily the owner of the house was refused permission to pull it down as he wanted to do, and three of the rooms upstairs had been unwillingly rented furnished, so that there were a number of tips and extras for Liza to earn. Otherwise we would have had to survive rather than live on what Liza gained from her caretaking.

As I turned the letters over I remembered how out of the unknown one at last arrived bearing a Spanish stamp with the postmark of some place on the Costa Brava. It contained a far more important sum than he had ever sent before – a cheque for three thousand pounds drawn on a bank in Switzerland – and I recalled Liza's exclamation of dismay. 'That's awful. What's he done? They'll catch him. They'll send him to prison for years and years.' But, if for no other reason, the lack of an extradition treaty at that time with Spain saved him from such a fate.

I found this letter near the top of the pile and I read it for the first time. It had arrived, I could tell by the date, not long before I left and went to work as an apprentice reporter on a local newspaper, having gained the job in spite of my youth by a very readable account of a bizarre accident which never really happened. Perhaps the title I gave the piece had caught the editorial attention – 'The Biter Bit'. I feared the editor might check up with the source which I falsely claimed, but I timed my piece well, the paper was just going to press, and the editor was anxious to get it in the first and only edition before the story could hit the headlines of the giants, the *Mail* or the *Express*. I had been innocent enough before then to share Liza's belief that what counted for a newspaper was truth rather than reader-interest, and my success helped to cure my innocence.

When I came to give the good news of my job to Liza – all the more good in my eyes because of the clever little bit of crookedness I had used (which I felt the Captain would have approved), I found her sitting in the kitchen with the letter I now held in her hand.

Though Liza had told me to destroy the letters, I had no intention of doing so, at least until I had read them all. Of course I would reassure her on my next visit to the hospital – 'never took them out of their envelopes – popped them straight into the oven'. I had no sense of guilt. These two people had made me what I had become. I had a right to know my creators.

'My dear Liza,' I began reading, 'I'm off again as soon as I can after this letter's posted. Spain isn't as good as it used to be, so I'm off where I always wanted to go, to the just republics where a man can make his fortune without fuss or bother, and it may be a little time before I write again and the letters may take rather a long time, so don't be anxious, I'm fighting fit, but I can't bear to think of you still living in that miserable basement year after year. It's time Jim got a job and contributed. Please use this cheque to find somewhere better. I wish the cheque was a bigger one, but I have to keep enough for my journey and finding my feet, though that won't take long I think where I'm going. As soon as I'm settled I'll give you my poste restante number and I swear that quite soon I'll be sending you another much bigger cheque, enough for you to join me in the place where I've settled. I miss you, and I need you, Liza, all these bits of years without you have been awful, and sometimes I can't sleep at night for worrying about you. Your letters don't tell me much. You were never one to complain even when that Devil hurt you. Do believe me that it won't be long now before we are together. As for Jim of course he can come with you, if he wants to. I don't like you to travel alone. Tell him I can hear the mule bells on the way – he'll know what I mean. Your Captain. PS. My hair is beginning to go. I'll soon be glabrous. It's always that way when I'm without you.' The word 'love' I noticed was still missing, and what the hell did 'glabrous' mean? I looked it up in a dictionary when I got back to my room and found as the answer 'smooth skinned'. It made some sense for once, unlike most of the long words he liked to use.

Liza had not shown me the letter then, but even after the years which had passed I could remember the wetness in her eyes on the day she received the cheque, and how she told me with a kind of despair, 'He writes such a lot of rubbish. I haven't any time for such nonsense.'

'You look unhappy,' I told her. 'Is it bad news?'

'Oh, it's only because I've been cutting up onions.

What on earth does he mean by hearing a lot of mule bells?'

'I suppose they have mules in Spain.'

'But he's off again from Spain, and he doesn't even say where he's going. And glabrous?' she added. 'What does glabrous mean? I never understand those grand words of his. But it's always been his way. He's an educated man.'

All the same she had cashed the cheque and given me a share, but she wouldn't leave her basement. 'I'm not going to live like a swell on him,' she once said. 'I'm keeping all I can till he rings on the door.'

As far as I knew she never received the new poste restante address for her reply, and after another year had passed she began to speak of him in the past tense as one who was dead. 'Even if he was in prison,' she said to me, 'he would have written to me somehow.'

I took the letters with my own unfinished scrawl back with me to the two-roomed flat for which I had exchanged my bed-sitting-room in Soho after I received a share of the cheque, and in the weeks which followed I read the letters several times. It was as though I were looking through someone else's eyes at the dying woman who had been my substitute mother, and as I seemed to peer at her between the lines, the mystery grew. What had kept those two so close and yet so strangely apart? Twice in my life after I left 'home', I had found myself in what I called love, and on each occasion the affair had ended (so far as I was concerned) quite happily, and I looked forward with increased confidence to some third girl whom I had not yet encountered. With both girls there had been, during brief absences, an exchange of what might be called, I suppose, love letters. (I had preserved the girls' letters as a proof of how successful I had been, and I imagined that the girls with equal pride had probably kept mine.) There was certainly no lack of the word 'love' in any of these letters, and there were plenty of references to the pleasures we had shared together, but when I read the Captain's letters I found myself entering a foreign land where the language was totally strange to me, and even when a word was identical to one in my own tongue, it seemed to have a quite different meaning.

'Last night I had a strange dream about you, Liza. You had come into a fortune, and you had bought yourself a car and the worst of it all was you were a very bad driver and I was sure you would have an awful accident and you would be in hospital again and I wouldn't know where. I woke up feeling you were far away so I'm writing this letter because there is no other news bad or good but this funambulist dream, but please go on hoping.'

This was an earlier letter than the one with the Spanish stamp. I looked up 'funambulist' too in the dictionary. I think he must have connected it with words like 'funeral' and 'funereal', for the true meaning 'rope-walker' certainly made no sense. He was not so educated as Liza thought.

Another letter began: 'Please, please, don't worry as I guess you are doing about the size of that cheque. I'm going to make a fortune one day which we'll share. Only perhaps it would be safer for you – because I don't want you to be worried by people asking questions again – if I make future cheques out to 'Bearer'. I wouldn't open an account if I were you – it's always better to keep money in cash and no one's going to rob your poor basement. The cheques will be signed for the time being Carver. I've never liked Cardigan – too honorifical – and I've had quite enough of Victor. Even Jim doesn't like that name and he has reason. But you don't need to worry, everything here is hunky-dory except for missing you. This is a dull business letter, but you know well enough the other things which I don't want to write today. You are my life, Liza, remember that. A man has got to have an object for living and you are my object. Your Captain. PS. I wish all the same you would leave that basement and not let the Devil have your address, only let the post office have it for forwarding. Don't reply to this letter until I let you have the poste restante of Carver because I think I may be moving around again.'

This must have been the last letter Liza received before she was taken to hospital; the postmark was indecipherable and the stamp was Colombian.

I took another letter at random. I felt that I was – for some reason valuable only to myself – in search of knowledge, and I remembered what my father had said about the Captain's lies. But what, I asked myself, had the Captain to gain from lying to Liza when he was so far away? When I lived together with a girl I had too often found the necessity of lying – to preserve the relationship a bit longer, but what sort of a relationship could remain intact when two thousand miles intervened? Why keep up such a comedy? Or was it a comedy which the Captain was playing to himself alone to escape from his loneliness? It was possible that the next letter of an earlier date which I chose to read did suggest a partial explanation.

'You are the only one besides myself I seem to have

been able to help a little. To so many I seem to have done only harm. I get frightened when I think that one day I may harm you too like I've harmed the others. I'd rather die now than let that happen – but then my death might be harming you even more than my life has done. Dear Liza, I can talk more easily on a bit of paper than I can with my tongue. Perhaps I ought to live in the next room to you and just write you notes?'

Why, I wondered, did the Captain feel this need always to be away from a woman he loved. Did he really fear the harm he might do?

'Sometimes when you wanted to talk to me the handle would turn and you would come in – if it was only to give me a cup of tea. How I would watch that handle to see it move, though the tea didn't suit me all that well. I drink only whisky now. It's better for the stomach, and tea which reminds me of you seems a bit too funambulist.' That word again.

As always there was a PS as though he were reluctant finally to fold the paper and put it in an envelope. 'Don't be scared, Liza. I'm only joking. One whisky at six o'clock. I'm not turning into a boozer. I can't. For the sort of work I'm doing I have to keep my wits dry as a bone.'

What work? I wondered. The word 'wonder' seemed to come only too often to my mind.

(2)

To me these were the oddest of love letters, if they were indeed love letters and not merely the expression of a deeply sentimental friendship. They aroused my curiosity. I had been reading one half of a shared life and I wanted to read the other half. What sort of a reply did the Captain receive at the other end of the world? Perhaps it was the old ambition to be 'a real writer' which was latent in me and the curiosity of a would-be writer which drove me next to go and speak to that family Devil, my father. I want to continue this account and find a better conclusion than 'I wonder perhaps.'

I had a good enough excuse – it was only right after all to tell him of Liza's serious state. But even if she had already died I would have seen no necessity to more than inform my father of her funeral – if you could call a funeral the half hour which I would have to spend at a crematorium, perhaps with two shopkeepers and one of the tenants, who sometimes asked her to do a bit of cleaning.

So it was that I wrote to my father, telling him nothing of Liza's state, for it might have robbed me of my only excuse for a meeting. I simply suggested that when next the Devil came to London, we should see each other. I had of course another reason. I was getting short of money. If Liza died I would have no claim on her 'estate' (I used the word to myself with irony), that unknown account into which she had perhaps against the Captain's advice more than once paid a cheque made out to 'Bearer'. If she had obeyed his instructions surely there would have been more than the few pounds I had found in the bedroom drawer, and yet there was no sign of a cheque book anywhere unless she had it with her when she was taken to hospital.

Before I had received a reply from my father, I went back to the basement and found another letter, which had been pushed under the door, carrying a stamp of Panama.

The Captain wrote: 'I enclose another of Carver's cheques to Bearer. This time for fifteen hundred pounds. It's not as much as I meant to send, but it's just enough for you to pack your bags and fly here to Panama City. There are two weekly planes from London, but you have to change at New York and I don't much like the thought of your going through New York, especially alone. There are good reasons not to. Better take a plane to Amsterdam and come direct from there. It's a long journey, so please travel first and take a glass or two of champagne to help you sleep. Telegraph Carver at Apt 361 Panama City date and time of arrival and the old man will be waiting impatiently for your plane to touch down. Don't worry about Jim. It's good for him to be on his own for a while and it won't be very long before he joins us. We'll see to that together. I have a job I think I can arrange for him here in a few weeks' time. Tell him the mules are heavy laden and very close now, but I can't wait for you to join me until then. I'll soon be a rich man, Liza, I swear it, and all I have will be yours and his. I'm so excited by your coming, I can't sleep. Come quickly and make Carver goluptious.' I think he judged words by their sound and this time when I got round to checking he proved to be not so far out.

I carried the letter and the cheque with me when I went to meet the Devil at the rendezvous which he had proposed at the Reform Club. I noticed how much my father had aged in the years that had passed since he intruded on the three of us accompanied by my unbearable aunt.

He greeted me at the bar with a reproach, 'Why didn't you tell me Liza was in hospital?' I answered back with equal harshness, 'I didn't think you would be interested. How did you know?'

'That aunt of yours – she always knew everything. Perhaps one of the tenants told her. I suppose you don't give the Devil credit for any human feeling.'

'Should I?'

'Oh, forget it. Have a drink. I suppose you do drink. After all you *are* my son.'

I was unused to anything but beer which was all that I could afford, but my mind switched suddenly back to the Captain on our first day together, and I said, 'A gin and tonic.'

'A large vodka for me,' my father told the barman and he added over his shoulder, 'When you are my age you will learn not to dilute good alcohol with fizz.'

'I didn't come here to learn how to drink.'

'What exactly did you come for? Money?'

'No, I'm managing. Just about managing.'

'And our friend – you know the one I mean – what does he call himself now? Is he very upset about Liza?'

'He's calling himself Carver at the moment, and he doesn't yet know about Liza. He's away somewhere in Panama.'

'Panama? So this time he's really put himself out of reach. What's he done to make him go that far?'

'He seems to be doing pretty well. I have a letter here which arrived with a cheque after Liza went to hospital. He wants her to join him – and me to come later.'

I gave the Devil the envelope.

My father said, 'These little countries always have such

pretty stamps. It's about all they've got to sell.' He added, 'There's no postmark. Someone brought it by hand.'

He led the way to a sofa where he sat and read the letter. He asked, 'Have you telegraphed Carver Apt 361?'

'Not yet. I've been wondering what to do with the cheque if Liza dies. Should I tear it up?'

'One should never tear up money,' my father said. 'Money is always good. Money has no morality. Better not telegraph him about Liza. He might stop the cheque.' He seemed to me more interested in the cheque, which he examined closely, than the letter. He went on thinking aloud, 'Made out to Bearer? One doesn't see that often these days. Why doesn't he put her name? Perhaps he thought the tax people would be after her. Or just for the sake of secrecy. He loved secrets.'

It was as if he felt pleasure from the feel of the cheque. 'Bank of London and Montreal. Address in Panama. I hope for your sake the London branch will accept it from you.'

'He meant it for Liza, not me.'

'He owed me fifty pounds. If you cashed the cheque, you could pay me back. Only fifty out of fifteen hundred.' The idea obviously amused him.

'It would be swindling him, wouldn't it?'

'And how do you think *he* came by the money. Earned it? I doubt if the Captain (that's the permanent name you both call him, isn't it?) I doubt if he ever earned any money honestly in his life. Come, let's have some lunch and consider very carefully this interesting moral point.'

For the second time I found myself beginning a meal with smoked salmon. The taste of it brought the Captain sympathetically close.

My father was silent (perhaps he was brooding on the question of morality), so in order to make conversation I inquired after my aunt's health.

'Could hardly be worse,' my father said. In the respectable surroundings of the Reform Club I thought it would only be good manners to lie. 'I'm sorry,' I said.

'In fact,' my father went on with relish, 'she died the day before yesterday. Just after she telephoned me about Liza being in hospital. She was a bitch to the last. She left you nothing – nor me either. Everything went to a home for stray dogs.'

'I wouldn't have expected anything from her. After all . . .'

'She was a good deal worse than her sister – I mean your mother, and that's saying a lot. You owe it to me she didn't put the police on your track all those years ago – only a private detective. I said I would fight any case she brought. I had the legal custody. So all she could do was try to prove with her detective that Liza wasn't capable. Luckily for you she failed at that.'

'And you lost me at chess – or was it backgammon? A fine father you were.'

'I knew you weren't happy with your aunt. And money was quite a problem for me then. I had been paying all the school fees, and there were other reasons. Liza is a good girl and she had wanted so much to have a child. Not me. One was more than enough. The doctor cost a lot and he did his job badly. As for the Captain – he's not such a bad fellow in his way. A bit of a liar, of course, and a bit of a cheat. You can't trust him where money's concerned, but who the hell can you trust when it comes to money? I was doing my best for both of you, leaving you with Liza, and you can't say it's worked out badly, not if the cheque's cashable. You'll be getting more from him than you were ever likely to get from me if you keep the cards close to your chest.'

'Were they all lies he told us?'

'I don't know which ones he told you. He always had a rather large repertoire.'

'How he escaped the Germans . . .'

'Well I suppose he must have escaped from them if he was ever a prisoner and I think he probably was.'

'He uses strange words. Usually when I look them up they don't make any sense.'

'He told me once that the only book he had to read in prison was half an English dictionary. The other half had been used as a bum wiper. Well, with a "goluptious" he seems to have read as far as the Gs.'

'Yes. And there are some Fs. Once he used a word I can't remember which means "rope-walker".'

'Any Hs?'

'I think there was one H.'

'I expect his half of the dictionary didn't get as far as J.'

'How did he escape?'

I hoped at least to hear again that story of the Pyrenees.

'He never went into details. Details are dangerous when you are lying. But I think he was pretty quick on his feet. You might say that's how we became acquainted.'

The waiter came to take our plates and for a while the menu absorbed him. He said, 'The cold roast beef is always good if you like it red as I do. And we can trust the house wine.' If money had once been a problem, it was a problem which he seemed to have solved satisfactorily.

'How was it you met?' I asked. It was the Captain who interested me – not my father.

'It was after your mother died. I can't pretend I missed her – we hadn't got on well for years. In fact not since your birth, which, if you forgive my saying so, was at the time a psychological mistake, as well as a bit of carelessness on my part. Well, after that, you might say that I looked around and began living with Liza though I wouldn't call it living, but sort of making the time pass. She was a nice girl, she knew it wasn't for keeps, and the surgeon was really to blame – though of course your aunt blamed me for what happened, and Liza was badly upset. I hadn't realized that she wanted the damned child so much – until she lost it.'

'I asked you about the Captain not Liza.'

'So you did. So you did. What does he call himself now?'

'You saw in the letter. Carver.'

'We'd better stick to the Captain. It's easier to remember. You want to know how I met him. I'm getting things a bit out of order. That's what lunch does to one. You'll find it when you get to my age. The mind wanders, and that's what happened to me over the chess game we played after a good dinner. Why did he say it was backgammon? Sometimes I think he lies just for the sake of lying. Or perhaps he wants to keep everything hidden.'

'Hidden from what?'

'Oh, I don't necessarily mean the police. Perhaps from himself. What were we saying?'

'You were going to tell me how you first met him.'

'Oh yes, as a matter of fact it was between Leicester Square and Covent Garden on the Underground. You might say a quite suitable place – the Underground. It was late, nearly midnight, and few people were around – in fact only myself waiting to get out, a man reading a newspaper and a boy – really a boy – he couldn't have been more than sixteen – who came up to me and said, "Your money or your life." (I suppose he'd heard that on television or in some child's mag.) I laughed and turned my back and there was a tinkle on the ground and a knife was lying there and a voice said, "Be off, you little bugger", and that, you see, was the Captain. Quick on his feet as I told you. He said to me, "The young ones are the dangerous ones. They don't think twice." Of course I thanked him and next day we met for a drink near the scene of action at the Salisbury in St Martin's Lane and there he said that he was coming up north to take on a job not far from me, so of course I invited him to spend a night. In fact he spent nearly a week with me then and he didn't seem in any hurry to take the job – if there was one. So that was how he met Liza. She was four months' gone and I never knew he was getting all that interested in her. She didn't exactly look her best. Well, you know how the story went.'

'I know very little.'

'She went off with him after the abortion. She must have written to him as soon as she got on her feet again. I must say it was a bit of a relief to me, for she wasn't fit for much when she came out of hospital.'

'You were lovers. It must have been a bit of a shock.'

'I wouldn't call us lovers – bedfellows. You ought to leave a word like lovers to the gossip columns. She had cheated me, trying to have a child. Perhaps she had marriage in mind, but I wanted none of that nonsense. I told her I'd treat her to an abortion, but I wouldn't pay for a child. One child was quite enough – you. That abortion of Liza's cost me a lot in those days when it wasn't strictly legal, and it was no fault of mine when things went wrong and she knew she could never have another. I suppose she felt a bit desperate and remembered the Captain. He had been very *convincingly* kind. He can be pretty convincing, especially when he's lying.'

'Weren't you jealous?'

'Jealous of poor Liza. Not on your life. Let me see that letter again.'

He read the letter more carefully than he had the first time. 'What the hell does he mean about the mules? He's not the type to take up farming.'

'I think . . . Of course I'm not sure . . . when I was a child he used to tell me about Drake – seizing the mule trains carrying gold across Panama.'

'Panama . . . gold trains . . . you don't really think . . . ?'

'Oh, I don't suppose there are any gold trains now. It's just the way of saying . . . well . . .'

'Well what?'

'I think he thinks . . .' It seemed to me that one 'think' almost immediately gave birth to another 'think'. 'Thinks' were breeding like rabbits – or that other word 'wonder'.

My father asked, 'And what is it you think?'

'I think he believes that he's about to make a lot of money.'

'I doubt if the Captain will ever do that. But to return to the cheque . . .'

'You think' (think again) 'that I should cash it? If she dies.'

'I wouldn't wait till then. You can look after the money better than poor Liza. But be careful. He's the sort of man who might prove dangerous. I don't know why I say that. A sort of instinct. And the way he handled that boy in the Underground. Underground. He's an Underground type himself.'

'All the same . . .'

'You've lived with the Captain long enough. Would *he* hesitate to cash a good cheque which might be stopped if there was any delay?' I pondered the point and thought the Devil had reason on his side.

As I left the club I asked him, 'Will you be visiting Liza?'

'No,' he said, 'it would do me no good and it certainly wouldn't do her any.'

(3)

I cashed the cheque after some trouble (I think they must have telephoned Panama and seven hours' difference in time can't have helped). I had a certain sense of guilt but one which was small enough to fade quickly after I paid my father his fifty pounds. I even treated myself on the strength of my new wealth to smoked salmon and a dry Bordeaux at a Soho restaurant which I couldn't normally have afforded, but all the same I found that I didn't enjoy my solitary meal as much as I had hoped. It was not because of the money; I believe it was the realization that I hadn't even yet written to the Captain to tell him that Liza was ill, probably dying.

Soon after this little celebration of mine another letter arrived marked Express. It was delivered just as I was sitting down to my breakfast of toast and tea, and I neither ate nor drank until I had read it twice over.

'My dearest Liza, perhaps after all you shouldn't come out here yet. There are difficulties – troubles – and I don't want you to feel any sort of unease. I hope that you've cashed the cheque that I sent because I can't send any more to you for the moment because of these difficulties. I'll be writing to you again as soon as I can and it won't be very long, I swear. Tell Jim not to worry either. The mules are on the way all right, but there are a few pot-holes on the route. Unexpected and sometimes deep pot-holes. I wish to God this wasn't such a business kind of letter, when all I want to write is how much I miss you. I miss you every hour of the day. But, Liza, it won't be long now, I'm sure it won't be long. Your Captain.' And then there was the inevitable postscript: 'Before you go to bed give me a thought.' He had written first, 'when you go to bed' and then changed 'when' into 'before' for some mysterious reason unless perhaps he was avoiding a sexual connotation. 'Together we were not often unhappy, were we?' It was a very modest claim, I thought, for a lover to make. If indeed he was a lover. This wasn't the sort of language that I associated with love. Perhaps they were the easy lies of a man bent on keeping a woman quiet and at a distance.

A comparison came to my mind and I took out from a file on my desk the rough draft of a letter which I had written a year ago. I always made a rough draft of a love letter, and this one was addressed to a girl I thought I loved at the time called Clara: I wondered – wondered again – whether the Captain had the habit too of making rough drafts and perhaps had sent the wrong version, for his letter read very much like a first effort which was not intended to be seen. There was after all nothing wrong about making a rough draft. When I wrote an article I made rough drafts. In both cases – a love letter or an article – I worked hard to produce the maximum effect on the reader. Even a poet, I told myself, made rough drafts and no critic condemned him for insincerity. A poet would often keep his rough drafts and sometimes they were published after his death. Judging from his final version, if this were a final version, the Captain's rough drafts, I thought, would be very rough indeed and unlikely to find a publisher.

I read my own letter with a certain nostalgia. It began 'Whenever I get into bed' (I was surprised how close that phrase was to what the Captain had written) 'I put my hand out and try to imagine that I am touching you where it pleases you most . . .'

Well, I thought, my letter certainly wasn't poetry – it was meant, however crude the expression, to excite myself and Clara too. In my own way I had written as sincerely as the Captain, perhaps even more sincerely. I had left nothing out for the sake of good taste. I had written to please the two of us, and to hell with good taste.

But why, I asked myself, do I feel so angry with the Captain? And I realized that what I felt now was a sense of shame when I compared the two letters. Was it because I no longer wanted to put my hand out to touch Clara when I went to bed and I no longer troubled even to write to her. I had left her – or rather we had left each other – a few weeks after I wrote that letter. In my experience love was like an attack of flu and one recovered as quickly. Each love affair was like a vaccine. It helped you to get through the next attack more easily.

I read the Captain's letter a third time. 'I miss you every hour of the day.' That sentence at least could not possibly be true, but why did the Captain persist in penning such sentimental lies when there was no benefit to be gained from them since he was far away in Panama and she was stuck in her Camden Town basement? For how many years had he been writing just such deceptive letters while I had only written my exaggerations for a matter of months. Who was the greater liar? Surely it was the Captain, who had been imprisoning Liza with his lies and robbing her of liberty as the price of her loyalty?

My irritation against the Captain remained, until I began to ask myself, is it only my envy speaking, the envy of someone who has never felt real love for anyone?

A message came. I went to the hospital. Liza had lapsed into a coma and she died the next day. There was nothing left to do but bury her. She had left no will: if she had money it was in some unknown account. I told myself that I owed her nothing when I had paid the necessary bills, and a few days later I sent a telegram to Carver at the mysterious sounding Apt and signed it Liza. Surely, I told myself, it was kinder to break the news myself to the Captain. The telegram read 'Jim has left for Panama. He will explain. Time of arrival, flight number, etc. Love.' I crossed out the word 'Love'. She was unlikely to use the word.

I was tired of hack journalism. My desire to be a writer revived. I even picked up and corrected this history which

I had written of my childhood. One day it might find a publisher. The end I could not foresee, but at least I think I can bring the story up to date, and this I have done. I shall continue it as I would a journal and who knows what conclusion I may give it when I find myself with the Captain in that unknown territory of Panama.

PART

III

8

I decided to follow the Captain's advice to Liza and I bought my ticket to Panama via Amsterdam. It would have been much easier and quicker for me, and no more expensive, to go by New York, but I thought it better to obey his instructions. He had talked of difficulties, whatever that might mean, and the word worried me a little through all the long journey: after the descent at Caracas, and during the interminable stop at Curaçao I stayed in the plane, working on this old book of mine to bring it up to date. I was disinclined to descend even for an hour into the unknown.

It was a twelve-hour journey in all from Amsterdam: there had been ice on the city canals when I arrived and there was snow on the fields outside when I left, and after that we moved steadily through the darkness towards the sun.

If it were possible for the Captain to read what I am writing now he would learn how much I have continued to wonder about him – he is to me an eternal question-mark never to be answered, like the existence of God, and so, as all theologians do, I continue to write in order to turn the question over and over without any hope of an answer. Now on this journey I hardly looked at anything but the manuscript on my lap and I left the earphones on the seat beside me when a film was being shown, for I needed silence to think, I needed it with a kind of greed.

The silent images did not disturb my thoughts, for they were always the same whenever I happened to look up at the screen: bearded men on horseback gunning down bearded men on foot and riding furiously on.

A liar and a crook, those were the names the Devil had come close to calling the Captain, without any trace in his voice of condemnation, as though he were describing, with scientific precision, an interesting form of human life, and yet it was on this liar and this crook that Liza and I had depended for years, and not once had he ever finally failed us. He was the nearest thing I had known to what I thought of as a father, even though I had never been conscious of needing a father and I believed I had done reasonably well without one. It was certainly not towards a father that I was flying now – it was towards a team of mules laden with gold riding along a rough track from the Pacific, it was towards adventure, and my mind, as the plane crossed the Atlantic coast of Panama, over the thick impenetrable forest of Darién, went back to the only other adventure which I could remember happening in my life. I felt again the same excited suspense which I had experienced as a boy when I waited outside the Swiss Cottage for the Captain to reappear: I was again staring at the logs in the timber yard beside the canal while the plane carried me, like the raft I had then planned to use, towards the Pacific ocean, where the city of Valparaiso must be standing with its feet in the sea and bearded sailors drank in bars. Now I was on my way to join them. It was as though I were reliving my life backwards towards that childhood dream on the day when I escaped from being an Amalekite for ever.

Then suddenly the plane slanted down towards a flat

blue liquid plain which I knew must be the Pacific. The forest yielded to the ruins of that old Panama which the pirate Morgan had destroyed and a few moments later the plane was rolling smoothly along the tarmac towards buildings which resembled any airport anywhere.

When I had passed through immigration and customs I looked around for the Captain, but there was nobody resembling him to be seen. My suitcase was heavy and I put it down. Not many passengers had got out at Panama (the plane went on to Lima) and soon I was quite alone in the hall, and I felt abandoned. Had my telegram to Apt not arrived? Or perhaps – it was only too likely – the Captain in the meanwhile had moved on elsewhere.

A good ten minutes must have passed as I stood there wondering what to do and where to go. I had begun to realize what a fool's journey it was that I had chosen, when a new figure appeared in the hall and after a little hesitation moved slowly towards me. I had time as he approached to think that I had never seen a taller and a thinner man. His trousers were like a second skin. He was narrow as well – narrow shoulders, narrow hips – even his eyes were too close together. He was like a caricature in a newspaper serial.

When he reached me he asked, 'Are you called Jim?'

'Yes.'

'Your plane,' he said in a tone of accusation as though I had been the pilot, 'was twelve minutes early.' I was to learn later how very careful he was about exactitude, especially with numerals. I don't believe he would even have trusted a computer to calculate so correctly. Anyone else would surely have said 'ten minutes early'.

'Yes.' I felt it necessary to apologize, 'I'm sorry.'

'My name is Quigly. I have been asked to meet you.'

There was a very slight American twang to his speech, a sort of echo from a distant land, something he might have picked up after too long a stay away from his native country, wherever that might be.

'Where,' I asked him, 'is the Captain?'

'What captain?' Before I could answer he added, 'Mr Smith told me to say he was sorry not to be here, but he had to go away for a while. He has booked a room for you.'

'Mr Smith?'

'He told me that he had received a telegram saying that you were coming.'

I assumed correctly that the Captain had changed his name once again, and this time to Smith. It seemed a rather humble name after Victor, Claridge or even Carver. I hoped for my own sake that he had not come down in the world.

'Will he be away long?'

'That I can't say. Two or three days? Two or three weeks?' (Figures again.) 'Mr Smith is a very busy man.'

'Do you work with him?'

He seemed to share the Captain's dislike for questions, for he made no answer to mine.

'If that's all your luggage we can be off.'

'Where to?'

'The Continental Hotel. You had better take your meals there. Mr Smith has arranged a credit.'

I can well understand the reason why my thoughts went nervously back to a suitcase containing two bricks, but the Continental proved a more important hotel than the Swan Inn and Mr Smith's reputation was certainly even higher, for I was greeted like a valued guest. In the lift to the fourteenth floor the receptionist inquired after both my journey and my health. Mr Quigly all the while remained silent. Outside the door of my room sat a young man who carried a revolver holster on his belt. 'This is your bodyguard,' Mr Quigly said in a voice which seemed to me to mark a certain disapproval.

'Why a bodyguard?'

'I understand that it was the wish of Colonel Martínez.'

'Who on earth is Colonel Martínez?'

'Oh, I leave that to Mr Smith to explain. I know nothing about such things.'

Then a dispute arose concerning a key which didn't fit my lock. We each of us tried it in vain.

'They've given me the wrong key or you the wrong room,' Mr Quigly said. He told the bodyguard, speaking in a Spanish simple enough for me to understand, 'Go and tell them. Find out which is the right room.'

The man replied that it was for Mr Quigly to go. He had his orders. The name Colonel Martínez cropped up again. He had to wait here. With Señor ... Señor ... He was my bodyguard. He had been told not to leave Señor ... He was obviously at a loss for the name.

I tried to convey in the little Spanish which remained to me from the Captain's lessons that I was prepared to go myself. I could see that they were both unhappy at the idea, and in the end all three of us descended from what had been numbered for superstitious reasons the fourteenth floor.

The mistake proved not to be the wrong key but the wrong room. The tag with the number had somehow come loose and been mislaid. An exactly similar room on an exactly similar corridor the floor below, number fourteen, superstition again, proved to be mine, and Mr Quigly exclaimed at the sight of the interior: 'Of course he's given you his own room. There's the stain on the carpet where I remember he spilt his drink. I suppose he wanted to keep the room safe from strangers in his absence.'

It was certainly large enough to house the two of us, I thought, if I used the sofa as a bed. Indeed I was surprised by the luxury of the room which seemed quite out of keeping with the Captain's character, though perhaps in the days when he called himself a colonel . . .

There was a bar and a refrigerator full of small bottles, and seeing these I suggested we might all have a drink. The bodyguard refused, perhaps for professional reasons as a taxi driver would, but Mr Quigly promptly accepted. With a drink in his hand he seemed to become a little more human. He settled himself on the sofa while the bodyguard remained standing like a sentry near the door. I felt more imprisoned than protected.

Mr Quigly drank his little bottle of whisky neat, but he didn't speak. He just licked his lips in a ruminating way. I went to the window and looked out over a great curve of the unknown city. I saw little but skyscraping buildings which seemed to compete with each other for height, and among them I counted four banks, and to make conversation I remarked to Mr Quigly, 'We seem to be in the banking quarter.'

'The whole city,' Mr Quigly said, 'is a banking quarter – except the slums. I believe that there are a hundred and twenty-three international banks.' Exact numbers again.

A long silence followed. I finished my own drink before I broke it. 'This must be a very expensive hotel, Mr Quigly.'

'There are no cheap hotels in Panama,' Mr Quigly replied with what I took to be pride rather than criticism.

I thought of the Captain's large cheque which had brought me here and his habitual phrase about the mule train. 'The Captain, I mean Mr Smith, must be doing pretty well,' I said.

'Don't ask *me* how he is doing. I wouldn't know. Ask Mr Smith,' and Mr Quigly gave a precautionary nod towards the bodyguard. 'I know very little of Mr Smith's activities.'

'And yet he asked you to look after me.'

'We are friends,' Mr Quigly replied, 'but not close friends. I can be of use to him occasionally and he appreciates that. I feel sure that in time our friendship will grow, for we have interests in common.'

'Mules?' I asked him.

'What on earth do you mean by mules?'

'Oh forget it,' I said. 'Have you any idea when he's returning?'

'None. But you have no need to worry. I told you – he has arranged a credit for you at the desk. As long as you remain in the hotel you need spend nothing. Just sign a chit.'

A great many years had passed since I last saw the Captain, but I remembered again that other chit which he had signed after the smoked salmon and the orangeade.

'And now,' Mr Quigly said, 'you must excuse me. I have to be off. Business calls. You will find my telephone number on this card and you can ring me if you have any problem.' He held out his long cold fingers for a shake, a quick dry shake, and I was alone with my bodyguard.

Luckily he proved to know a little English and this I could supplement with my own small amount of Spanish, and we both of us in the hours we spent together soon improved our linguistics. This was fortunate for during the next few days he proved to be a very close companion. I liked him a good deal more than I had liked Mr Quigly. We took our meals in common in the hotel restaurant where the waiters dressed as sailors served seafood and the walls were decorated with ropes. The fact that Pablo carried a gun seemed to arouse no more curiosity than the sailor suits; the revolver might have been part of the same romantic decor which, I thought, suited the Valparaiso of my childish dream. It was on our second day that I felt our companionship could afford a frank question. 'Pablo,' I asked him over my glass of Chilean wine, 'why are you guarding me?'

'The orders of Colonel Martínez.'

'Who is this Colonel Martínez?'

'My boss.' He used the English word.

'But why? Am I in some danger?'

'Señor Smith,' he said, 'has a number of enemies.'

'Why? What is he up to?'

'That you must ask him when he returns.'

But many days were to pass before then. To escape boredom I asked Pablo not only to guard me – from what? – but to show me his city. It was a city of steep hills and torrential rainstorms which lasted for less than a quarter of an hour and yet made miniature Niagaras down the streets, leaving cars stranded. It was also a city of slums as Mr Quigly had mentioned to me, not only of banks. In the quarter which was called ironically Hollywood it was a shocking contrast to see the tumbledown shacks on which the vultures lodged and in which whole families were crowded together in the intimacy of complete poverty only a few hundred yards from the banks, where the high windows glittered in the morning sun, and it was even more of a shock to gaze into the American Zone across the mere width of a street, and see the well-kept lawns and the expensive villas on which no vulture ever cared to settle. On our side of the road which was called the Street of the Martyrs, and had been named, Pablo told me, after some old conflict between American Marines and students, it seemed I was subject to Panamanian law, while on the other side I would be in the American Zone and I could be hauled away there for any infringement of the American law and tried in New Orleans. More and more I wondered what had induced the Captain to settle in this city, for there were no signs of any gold outside the coffers of the international banks and I doubted his capacity to break a bank.

One day Pablo took me for a drive the whole length of the immaculate green Zone. I felt all the more astonished that such riches could exist in sight of such poverty without any customs officer or frontier guard to keep the inhabitants of Hollywood from breaking in. I forget what words I used to express my amazement, but I remember Pablo's reply. 'This is not only Panama. This is Central America. Perhaps one day . . .' He patted the holster at his side. 'One needs better weapons than a revolver, you understand, to change things.'

Sharing meals with my guardian I came to know and like him more and more, and as my liking grew I found that we could wander in our talk beyond the tidy zone of discretion. I could tell how well he knew the Captain, for it had been his job to guard him just as he now guarded me. It was the unknown Colonel Martínez who had given him his orders. He referred to the Captain always as Señor Smith and I adopted the name.

As we were driving through the American Zone to see a little of the more rural Panama which existed on the other side of this non-existent frontier I asked him abruptly, 'Who are Señor Smith's enemies?', and his reply was a silent one – a wave of his hand towards the golf house and a putting green and a group of officers in immaculate American uniforms, watching the players. He wouldn't enlarge on his gesture, as though he considered that he was betraying nothing of his employer's secrets so long as he didn't employ any spoken term.

Every day he remained with me till bedtime and I never discovered where it was he spent the nights. Certainly not outside my door, for I had looked out there. Perhaps he trusted me not to take to the streets after I said goodnight since he had warned me that they were not safe after dark. 'Not so bad here as in New York,' he told me, 'but bad, very bad all the same. What can you expect where people are so poor?' There were the makings of a real revolutionary in Pablo, I thought, given the right leader.

Mr Quigly remained much more of a mystery to me. I could feel an antagonism between him and Pablo and I instinctively sided with Pablo. At least he carried his weapon unconcealed, but I doubted whether Mr Quigly in his tight North American clothes could have found room for that kind of a weapon. I wondered why the Captain had arranged for Mr Quigly to meet me –

perhaps it was because his language was English and the Captain, who had been my teacher, knew how weak my Spanish was. Mr Quigly would call on me regularly around eight-thirty in the morning, if only to speak to me about nothing in particular, usually on the telephone in the hall below. The first time he had explained the early hour by saying that he was on his way to his office, which was not far from the hotel. This gave me the chance of asking him what he did. A small hesitation was conveyed up the line. 'I am a counsellor,' he replied.

'A counsellor?'

'A financial counsellor.'

I thought immediately of the Captain's mule trains and I asked, 'Do you deal in gold?'

'There is no gold in Panama,' he replied. He added, 'There never was any gold. That was a legend. The gold came from elsewhere.'

Our brief conversations always concluded with his question whether I had any news yet of Mr Smith's return, but I had none to give.

As my friendship with Pablo grew, I ventured a question or two on the subject of Mr Quigly. 'I don't understand him. He's not the sort of person I would expect my father to trust.' (I had accepted the story that Mr Smith was my father since I found the relationship was assumed by both Mr Quigly and Pablo. My passport, of course, bore the name of Baxter, but they probably imagined that my mother had married twice.)

'Señor Smith does not trust him very much I think,' Pablo replied.

'Then why did he ask Mr Quigly to meet me at the airport?'

Pablo had no solution to that problem.

About a week after my arrival Mr Quigly unexpectedly invited me to dinner. That night he was a changed Mr Quigly, and not only in mood. He was almost physically changed for he was now wearing a jacket with padded shoulders which made him look flatter but less narrow, and his trousers seemed less tight. He made an obscure joke which I didn't understand, though he laughed or rather giggled at it himself. His friendship with the Captain became to me even more inexplicable.

He told me, 'I am taking you to a Peruvian restaurant. The Pisco Sours are excellent there.'

'Is Pablo not coming with us?'

'I have told him that I will be your bodyguard this evening. I have promised not to let you out of my sight.'

'What about Colonel Martínez?'

'I gave Pablo a little tip just for once and he agreed to forget the Colonel. A tip goes a long way in Panama, even in some very high circles.'

'Do you too carry a gun?'

'No no. In my case there is no danger. They consider me an honorary Yankee, and no one, at this moment especially, would want any harm to come to a Yankee.'

I had never drunk a Pisco Sour before and when we had each drunk three I felt quite clearly the effect they had. Even Mr Quigly became almost jovial.

'No news from your good and errant father?' he asked.

The Pisco Sours had confused me. 'Oh, the Devil never writes,' I told him.

'I wouldn't have gone so far,' Mr Quigly said, after what seemed a calculated consideration, 'as to call him exactly a devil. A little mischievous sometimes perhaps.'

I thought it best not to explain the misunderstanding. 'Oh, devil is just a joke in the family,' I explained.

'I get on very well with him, but of course I can't share all his ideas.'

'Can one say that of anyone?'

He evaded my question. 'Perhaps another Pisco Sour?'

'Will it be wise?'

'One can't always be wise, can one, in a world like this?'

That night I found myself as near as I ever came to liking Mr Quigly. He seemed to grow less narrow in face and body with every Pisco Sour I took.

'Do you plan a long visit?' was the most direct question which Mr Quigly put to me and by that time we had abandoned the Pisco Sours and were deep into a bottle of Chilean wine. In the short intervals between our drinks he had spoken a little like a hired guide, recommending me to visit the Cocos Islands with their Indian inhabitants, who wore gold – gold? – earrings, and the Washington Hotel in the American Zone of Colón where he could vouch for the rum punches which were not reliable on the Pacific side of Panama. And then he told me that in the north there was a charming little resort in the mountains if I wished to take a weekend away ('I could arrange you special terms') and, how was it, he demanded, that he had nearly failed to mention one of the rarest attractions of Panama, the golden frogs which could be seen in a place the name of which I have forgotten quite a short ride on the other side of the American Zone. His conversation became more and more like a handbook for a tourist, a description of myself which I resented.

'But I don't regard this as a holiday,' I said. 'I am hoping to find a job.'

'Perhaps with Mr Smith?'

'Perhaps with Mr Smith,' and I quickly corrected myself, 'with my father.'

'I've never quite made out what your father does, but he seems to have good relations with the National Guard. Judging by Colonel Martínez giving you your own bodyguard.'

Mr Quigly changed the subject back to the tourist handbook and he spoke of an island called Toboso which was well worth a visit, where no cars were permitted and there was a long forgotten cemetery of Anglo-Saxons buried somewhere in the jungle. Only when we had finished the wine did he become personal again. He told me, 'I work here for an American paper. As a financial consultant. Panama is very useful as a centre of news for the whole Central American scene – there's a lot happening these days – in Nicaragua, Guatemala, El Salvador, a great deal of trouble everywhere. The way things are going my paper is glad to have a correspondent who is not strictly American. Luckily I have a British passport, though I left England when I was sixteen. Americans are not very popular in these parts because of the Zone. Mr Smith told me that you too have been in journalism.'

'I had a job on a very local paper,' I said, 'and I walked out without notice.'

'So they won't take you back, I suppose? A bit of a gamble, wasn't it, joining your father?'

The wine was making me confidential. Perhaps, I thought, I have been a bit unfair to Mr Quigly. 'Judging from his letters there's a lot of money to be made here. Of course he has always been a bit of an optimist.' I added carelessly, 'So long as I've known him.'

'Since you were a baby in fact?' Mr Quigly commented with the first hint of humour he had ever shown.

I decided after all to be truthful – perhaps that was the way the wine worked too. 'He isn't my real father,' I admitted, 'he's a kind of adopted one.'

'That is most interesting,' Mr Quigly replied, though I could not see what interest my bit of family history could possibly have for him. Perhaps he read a question in my eyes, for he added, 'At least with an adopted father like that you won't have to worry about the very unjust statement in what I like to call the Unholy Bible – "The sins of the fathers are visited on the children."' He giggled at the last drop which remained in his glass of Chilean wine. It was as though he had at last found an opportunity to use a joke which he had been keeping a long time in store, and I think he was disappointed by my failure to laugh. 'Perhaps,' he said, 'we could use another bottle of this Chilean brew.'

'Not for me. I've had all I can take.'

'Ah, a wise man. I think perhaps you are right, though all the same . . .'

This seemed a moment when I too could take advantage of the wine to extract a little information. 'I've wondered,' I said, 'why my father – let's call him that – asked you to meet me.'

His answer was what I had expected when I talked to Pablo. 'He thought your Spanish might not be good enough to cope with the bodyguard. You see with my journalistic contacts I've been able to help him now and then. He's had his difficulties too, though not linguistic ones.'

I remembered how the Captain had warned Liza against taking the easier and less expensive route to Panama via New York.

'With the Americans?'

'Oh, and others too. As I told you, I don't know exactly what business he is in.'

'He has an expensive room at any rate.'

'You can't judge by that. There are activities here where it pays well to look expensive in the short term. I do sincerely hope you will find he can find a place of work for you which you will find suitable. And rewarding. To be rewarding after all is the greatest thing.'

Mr Quigly looked at his watch and said with his usual precision: 'Ten seventeen.' Then he called for the waiter and asked for the bill, which he signed after a careful study of the figures. He even questioned the number of Pisco Sours. 'On expenses,' he told me and giggled again. 'Before we say goodnight,' he added, 'I would like to say how much I've enjoyed your company. A fellow Englishman. One does feel sometimes in these parts a little lonely. It's good to hear one's own tongue spoken.'

'Surely you have plenty of Americans close by in the Zone.'

'Yes, yes, but it's not quite the same, is it? I do want to tell you — it's not only the Chilean wine that speaks — if you have any difficulty in finding a job I might be able to help a little. Or if you need a bit of supplementary work. With me a story sometimes breaks suddenly, and I can't always be on the spot. I could do with an assistant. What I believe in the newspaper world you come from they call a stringer. Half time, half time at most. Of course I don't want to interfere with any arrangements Mr Smith may have made for you.'

At the door of the hotel he told me, 'You have my telephone number. Just get in touch with me at any time,' and something in the tone of his voice made me feel that he was disclosing at last the whole object of our evening together. But he need not have expended so many Pisco Sours in the course of it. I was only too well aware that I might need help when the Captain learnt that Liza was dead.

(2)

Two evenings later, when I was tired of walking the streets of Panama with Pablo and passing a dozen or more banks out of the hundred and twenty-three (I had no desire to return to the slums of Hollywood where we had been pursued by an addict wishing to sell us drugs for dollars), my bodyguard left me in my room, but he returned a moment later with the news that Mr Smith had arrived, that he would be at the hotel in half an hour, and that his guardianship was over. 'Señor Smith can look after you now. Colonel Martínez has withdrawn me.'

It was a good many years since I had last seen the Captain, and I felt as though I were waiting for a stranger or indeed a character existing only on the pages of that youthful manuscript of mine, on which I am still working. He existed there better on paper than in memory. For example if I tried to remember the occasions when he had taken me to a cinema it was only *King Kong* which came to my mind because I had recorded that memory in writing. When I thought of his previous arrivals after a long absence – only too frequent during our life together – it was the unexpected one with a bearded face which I saw in my mind's eye, because I had described it in words, or the stranger talking to the headmaster, the one who had afterwards fed me with smoked salmon. It was again because I had tried to recreate this character in my sorry attempt to become a 'real writer'.

So now, when the door of the room opened, I felt myself back in the Swan Inn and I was watching for a much younger man who would ask for his suitcase containing two bricks to be sent up to his room. I would not have been in the least surprised to learn that the suitcase which he planted heavily down on his bed contained similar bricks: what surprised me was the age of the Captain – the worn pleated old man's face. He wore neither a beard nor a moustache, and their absence seemed to give more room for the deep criss-cross lines in the skin, and the hair on his head was grey where it wasn't white.

'Why, Jim,' he said holding out an obviously shy hand, 'it's good to see you again after all this time, but I wish you weren't here alone.' He almost echoed my own thoughts when he said, 'What a lot older you look.' He added, 'It's odd, isn't it, that Liza's not here to make us a cup of tea, but then I suppose the time has come now when you'll be wanting something stronger. Whisky? Gin?'

'Your friend Mr Quigly has been teaching me to drink Pisco Sours, but I would prefer whisky.' (Remembering the long ago past I nearly said 'gin and tonic'.)

The Captain went to the bar. 'Quigly is an acquaintance,' he told me, 'he's hardly what I'd call a friend,' and as he prepared the two whiskies, he asked with his back turned to me, perhaps in order that I should not see the anxiety in his eyes, 'How's Liza?'

I don't think anyone can really blame me for not replying then with the simple truth, 'She's dead', and it was perhaps at that precise moment I dangerously decided to delay telling him of her death as long as I could.

After all I owed him nothing. Hadn't his only interest in me lain in his desire to give Liza what she couldn't otherwise have – a child? But I realized very well what difficulties remained for me to face. I had no idea of how often she was in the habit of writing to him and how could I explain her complete silence? I knew that inevitably, sooner or later, the truth was bound to come out, but somehow I had to establish myself first safely in this strange world before he knew that I had lied to him.

I said, 'Not too well.'

'What do you mean?'

'She had a small accident. Knocked down. On the way to the baker's. She had to go to hospital.'

'What sort of accident?'

I gave him a modified version of the truth without the sequel.

'And you've come here, leaving her alone in hospital . . . ?'

I nearly told him, 'She's used to being alone,' but I stopped in time when he added, 'You are the only companion she has.' I remembered that she had never written to tell him of my desertion, for fear of worrying him, nor would she have wanted to bring any pressure on him to

(127)

return. So I continued to lie carefully. 'She urged me to come. She gave me the money for the fare because she couldn't come herself. She plans to follow me. As soon as the doctors give the OK.' The lies and the evasions began to multiply and I found it impossible to check them.

'But I wasn't expecting her to come. I wrote to her not to come yet. To wait a little longer. Because of difficulties.'

'She thought I might be of help to you.'

'I hate the thought of her staying there in hospital – ill and alone.'

'She's probably back home by this time.'

'Yes. Home as you call it. In that dreary basement.'

'She was happy there. In her own way. Waiting for you to return.'

'Thank God she had you, but now . . . If only I could take the next plane back to Europe, but I can't. I've promised . . . In a month perhaps I'll be free, I'm almost sure of that, but a month is a hell of a long time for someone who is sick and alone.'

He took a long drink at his whisky. 'You always used to get the bread for her. Where were you when the accident happened?'

'I was working.'

'Oh yes, of course. You got that job on a paper. She wrote to me how glad she was that you weren't hanging around all day. It was something she enjoyed, looking forward to the evening when you came home.'

I had never thought before of quite how far he had been deceived by both of us. Together we had dug a hole which would hide the truth deeper than any grave. But there was one truth which sooner or later had to be unearthed – the truth of her death. She couldn't remain credibly silent to his letters for ever. I drank, but the whisky didn't help me to unravel that riddle.

The Captain poured himself a second glass of whisky. 'I don't drink tea any more,' he said, 'not that I ever really liked it. Tea for me belongs to only one place in the world, her place.' He was, I think, trying to ease the tension between us which he probably attributed to our different anxieties, perhaps even a change in our relationship. We were no longer a man and a boy – he was a much older man and I had altogether ceased to be a boy. He asked, 'What did you think of the man Quigly?'

'I couldn't make him out. I wondered why you sent him to meet me.'

'Pablo knows very little English, and I thought your Spanish – well, we never got very far with that, did we? At least Quigly would be able to explain things a bit to you.'

'He explained nothing.'

'I just meant about the hotel, this room, how you should put things on account, and what's best to eat in this benighted city. I wasn't able to meet you. I was on an important job. I was badly needed.'

'Not by the police?' I asked, meaning only to make light of that ambiguous past which Liza and I had shared with him.

'Oh no, it's not the police I have difficulties with now.'

'But there are still difficulties?'

'There always are. I don't mind difficulties. Life wouldn't be worth living without them. I'm afraid you've only got that sofa there for a bed now that I'm back.'

'I got used to a sofa in Camden Town. And it wasn't as comfortable as the one here.'

'I suppose this time you've got a pair of pyjamas?'

I was glad that his thoughts too were going back to that far past about which I had written. In the past there were no traps to be avoided, and each could talk freely to the other. 'They are not orange ones, thank God,' I said.

'But you put up with the orange ones the first night.'

'As soon as the house was quiet I took them off and went to sleep naked.'

'And rumpled them up I suppose so that Liza wouldn't notice?'

'I managed to tear them badly. In case I would have to wear them again after a wash.'

'Yes, I remember Liza was furious because I had to pay for another pair. I wasn't the only one with a double life, and you began yours even younger than I did.'

'But you've continued to live one,' I said. 'What *is* your job?'

'I'm not sure it's quite safe for you to know as yet.'

'Safe for whom?'

'For both of us.'

'Does Mr Quigly know?'

I was reluctant to leave out the title Mister when I spoke of Quigly. It seemed to distance me from the man. It was almost like an adjective of contempt.

'Oh, he'd like to know, but you can never trust a journalist if that's what he is.'

'I was a journalist a week ago.'

'Not a journalist of Quigly's kind, I hope.'

'What *is* Mr Quigly's kind?'

'He calls himself a financial correspondent, but he's hungry for all kinds of copy. I'm not sure that he always uses it for his paper. He's a man you have to watch.'

'Do you want *me* to watch him? Is that the job you have in mind for me?'

'Perhaps. It might be. Who knows? Anyway it's too late to talk now and we're tired. Let's have one more whisky and then go to sleep. At least *you* can sleep. I want to write first to Liza and tell her you've arrived safely.'

For a moment I could have believed that he was testing me, to see how long I would continue with my lie that she was alive, but of course it was not the case. He added, 'I always try to write to her before I sleep, even if I don't always send the letter. When the day is finished I can forget the difficulties and think only of her,' and it was to the sound of his pen on paper that I eventually fell asleep.

(3)

It was a chance, or so I thought it to be at the time, that I fell in with Mr Quigly the very next morning. When I woke the Captain's bed was empty, and on the chair beside it lay the letter to Liza still unsealed and un-stamped, perhaps because he meant to continue it after his work – what work? – the next evening or not send it at all. I was only momentarily tempted to read it – I had read so many of his letters recently that I could almost guess the contents of this one. It would surely contain the same unconvincing sentimentalities. All the same I felt a little proud of myself for refraining. It seemed to reduce a little my sense of guilt for my great lie.

I had hardly left the hotel, with no other purpose than to pass the time, when Mr Quigly appeared walking towards me. As the four banks were within a hundred yards the coincidence was easily explicable — in fact it was explained in just that way by Mr Quigly. 'Been drawing some expenses in red ink,' he said, 'and I've included you among them.'

'Me? I don't understand.'

'I would like to pay you a very small advance.'

'For what?'

'You can be of help with a news story I'm writing for my paper.'

'I don't see how.'

'As one journalist to another.'

'Has this something to do with' (I hesitated at the name) 'Mr Smith?'

'Not directly.'

'I'm sorry,' I told him, 'I can't help you,' and I walked away in a thoroughly bad mood without taking his money.

(4)

As I write this account I begin to realize that there is one great gap in my story. Surely I should have felt some grief for Liza's death. She had played her role as substitute mother very correctly over all the years after my unexpected arrival with the Captain — with what had seemed a natural affection and even a natural irritation on occasion — and with far more skill than my aunt had ever shown. I could make no complaints of the life I had led with her. The Captain believed she had needed a child to complete her happiness and to ease the loneliness he assumed she must feel during his many absences. Perhaps he had done wrong – perhaps he had only added a responsibility. How can one ever be sure of what another feels? Certainly she had never been possessive and even as a child I may have appreciated that, if only half consciously. It was this attitude of hers which enabled me to cut loose without scruples when my time for independence came, though I continued to play the comedy of a dutiful son by visiting her once a week – if nothing more attractive presented itself. Now I have to face the truth of that gap in my story. When they told me at the hospital that she was dead I felt no more emotion than when I had left her behind after a weekly visit to go to my bed-sitting-room in Soho. If there was any emotion it was the emotion of relief, a duty finished.

One object she did abandon in the hospital – it was a letter addressed only with the name of the Captain, for she had probably forgotten the Apt number which neither of us understood. I nearly opened it, but a cold sort of reason prevented me. I was going to the Captain: I couldn't present him with an open letter and I thought that handing the letter to him might be a way of breaking the news of her death and even excusing my use of his cheque to join him. But it was too late now and I had torn it up unread and put the scraps into a dustbin outside the hospital.

(5)

It was rash of me to have dismissed Mr Quigly so abruptly, for I was bored with my long solitary days in this city to which I was a stranger. I would even have welcomed the return of Pablo and, if the Captain was supposed by the mysterious Colonel Martínez to have taken the office of my guardian, why was he now absent so soon after his return? Anyway what on earth was the purpose of a bodyguard? I could feel no danger among the international banks when I changed a little of my money at one of them – or rather the remains of Liza's. Bodyguards and banks didn't seem to belong to the same world as mine or the Captain's. Perhaps only Mr Quigly would be at home among them both.

As it happened I wasn't to be left alone for very long. The Captain even apologized for his absence when he walked into our room. 'There were a few problems to be solved,' he told me. 'Now we can enjoy ourselves with a free mind and I will show you some of the beauties of Panama.'

'Please not the banks. Not the slums. I've seen too much of both. Are there any beauties?'

'The beauty of ruins,' he told me. 'They do teach us a lesson.'

'What lesson?'

'To tell you the truth – I'm not quite sure what.' The phrase 'to tell you the truth' was a key phrase with the Captain. How often Liza and I had exchanged ironic looks at the sound of it, for truth and the Captain were not easily paired. All the same, perhaps in this case he *was* looking for a true answer, since he stood a long while in respectful silence among the seaside ruins of the old city which Sir Henry Morgan had destroyed more than three hundred years before.

'You call these beautiful,' I said to break the silence.

'What are they but a lot of broken stones?' I had never before known him to be as silent as this.

'What did you say?'

'You think these ruins beautiful? Of course I suppose they *are* a lot better than all those skyscraper banks, but beautiful?'

'Think,' the Captain said, 'of all the work in those days which went into making these buildings into ruins. What a waste of time it was. Now I could have broken up this church in a matter of seconds – if it is a church.'

'How?'

'From the air with a couple of bombs.'

'If you had a plane. Sir Henry Morgan hadn't.'

'As a matter of fact' (it was not 'to tell you the truth' this time) 'I do have a little plane. Second-hand of course.' Was the word 'fact' the same to the Captain as the word 'truth' and just as little reliable, I wondered, and I said nothing in reply.

'I prefer Drake to Morgan,' the Captain continued, gazing, as it seemed to me, with a certain gloom at the ruins. 'Drake got the gold and killed a few Spaniards, but he didn't destroy a city. Why, I can show you the Spanish treasure house in Portobello exactly the same as it was in his day.'

'But what about your plane?'

'Oh, forget it. I didn't mean to tell you about the plane. It just slipped out. No importance. A silly hobby of mine. A man has to have a hobby.'

A plane to me seemed a very expensive hobby and I was left wondering how he had paid for it. Had he again signed a bit of paper?

What he had called a slip proved that evening to be

rather more important than I expected, when our conversation turned in a very dangerous direction. All had gone well at the start. The past was an area of safety, and we seemed to be harmlessly engaged in discovering each other in a friendly way after the years of absence.

I even probed just a little way into those dubious years and the unexplained visits of the police which I so well remembered. 'Do you remember that time when you were away for months and then you came back with a beard?'

He laughed. 'Yes, I had them foxed all right that time.'

'And then there was a report in the *Telegraph* . . .'

'What a memory you have.'

'Well, you see, some years ago I wanted to be a writer and I wrote a lot of what had happened down. After Liza's accident I found the manuscript and read it. About that robbery and the man the police were looking for.'

'"A man with a military bearing". Yes, I read that report too. It tickled me no end. They wouldn't say the same of me now would they, and yet in my way I'm a fighting man again. Those were good days even when they were a bit difficult. I worked with three others then. They weren't reliable, and they cheated when they could, but I had no choice of partners. I had to take what I could. I wanted to get Liza out of that dreary basement and give her a proper home, and it hurts me to think she will have to go back there from the hospital.'

I tried to interrupt the risky train of his thoughts. 'So you *were* that man in the *Telegraph*?'

'Of course I was.'

'And they wanted you for theft?'

'When you are talking of nearly three thousand pounds' worth of jewels it's not theft, it's robbery.'

'You were a robber then?'

'Like Drake before me. Drake not Morgan. I didn't destroy cities. I never did anybody any real harm.'

'What about the jeweller?'

'Why, he came to no harm at all. We were very careful when we tied him up. He was doing badly and he must have been glad of the insurance money. Those fellows are always very well insured. Anyway it was something I had to do.'

'Why?'

'I had my responsibilities. Liza and you.'

'Did Liza know?'

'She's a clever girl and I think perhaps she guessed a lot. I didn't have many secrets from her. Only small ones to stop her worrying. All I ever want is for her to be happy and one day I swear she will be.'

'Why did you keep on changing your name?'

'It used to be more of a joke than serious in those days. Even when I was a small boy I always wanted to make fun of coppers. I don't like coppers.'

I asked with real interest this time, 'What name did you have when you were born?'

'My name was Brown.'

I said with amusement, 'And now it's Smith. You are getting closer to the truth, the simple truth.'

'Well, this time it's my friends who have chosen the name for me. They wanted something they could remember. They found Carver difficult, but Smith is a bit difficult too – to pronounce. Latins don't like the th.'

He got up to pour two more whiskies. 'I'm talking

much more than I should. It's because I've been so bloody alone for too long.'

'Who are those friends of yours?'

'Good fellows. I try to help them, but we try not to see too much of each other. We are on to something of real importance now and each one of us works most of the time alone. Except for those who do the real fighting . . .'

'To get those mule trains?'

'That's right – the mule trains.'

'And is Mr Quigly concerned?'

'Leave Quigly out of it. I wouldn't trust him far.'

'I get the impression that neither of you trusts the other. Why are you friends?'

'I told you – not friends. It's a game. A serious game – like chess or backgammon. We swap pieces – unimportant pieces – though of course everything in a sense can lead to something important. For his friends or mine. Come along. Finish your whisky. It's time for bed – I mean the sofa. I'll just add a line or two to Liza. It's a habit I never want to lose.'

I lay down, but I didn't sleep for a long while. I lay and watched the Captain writing a line and then stopping, writing another line and stopping, more like a child doing a difficult exercise than a man corresponding with a woman he loved, a woman who was dead.

(6)

It was his mention of the plane which had intrigued me most and I thought that talking about the plane might help to delay the moment when some chance would reveal to him that Liza was dead. It might be that even Mr Quigly could be of assistance there. When I woke the Captain had gone again with only a small note left behind to tell me to charge my meals, or if possible anything I might want to buy, to the hotel. 'I shall be back before dark. Just a short fuliginous flight.' He included a hundred dollars in the envelope, and I was reminded of the mysterious remittances which in my childhood would come to Liza after the coded signal had sounded at the door. I felt no gratitude – I was even infuriated, for I had no wish to spend his money. I would much rather earn it myself in some way, even from Mr Quigly. I had no address, for the card had given only his telephone number. Even the Captain's misuse of that absurd word fuliginous irritated me.

In my anger I ordered the biggest breakfast I could think of on the telephone and left half of it uneaten. Then I went down into the hall of the hotel and saw Mr Quigly rising from a seat beside the door. 'Why, what a happy coincidence,' he said, 'I just dropped in here to take a little rest. In this heat . . . Is your father at home?'

'A hotel is not a home,' I said. I was still in a black mood. I added, 'He's on what he calls a short flight.'

'Ah, those flights of his. It's quite difficult sometimes to get hold of him.'

'Do you want to get hold of him?'

'Oh, I always like to have a chat with him. He has ideas of his own which interest me. Even when we disagree.'

I showed him the Captain's note. 'What on earth does fuliginous mean?' Mr Quigly asked.

'I knew once, but I've forgotten. I don't carry a dictionary around. Anyway a dictionary wouldn't help. I think he cares only for the sound. He gets the meanings wrong.'

I told Mr Quigly the story which the Devil had told me of the prison camp and the half-destroyed dictionary. 'He doesn't often use words like that when he speaks, but they seem to get control when he writes.'

'Like a poet?'

'Not much of a poet.' But then suddenly I thought, can it be from the Captain I have somehow inherited this irritating desire to be a writer? It certainly wasn't from the Devil or from my mother, and I began to feel a certain shame that I might be betraying to Mr Quigly one who had perhaps in a sense fathered me. Didn't I a bit resemble, in my desire to find words, the Captain in his perpetual search for the mules which carried gold?

Mr Quigly interrupted my thoughts. 'You know I was half planning to look you up,' he said. 'I was in touch with my paper yesterday and they have agreed in principle' (he emphasized the word principle) 'that I take you on as a stringer – for six hundred dollars a month payable on the first of the month – the arrangement to be terminated by either of us at any time without notice.'

'I don't understand. For doing what?'

'Oh, little stories will probably come your way which can fit into the end of a column. Sometimes I have to go off for a few days and then I would ask you to keep an eye on things. In a place like this a story can suddenly break. Panama is a curious place. A little capitalist state with a socialist general, split in two by the Americans. You and I as Englishmen can understand the difficulties which might arise here. It's as though England were split between the north and the south with the Americans in between. Somehow the Americans can't understand the resentment, because they bring in a lot of money. Panama would be poor without them, they expect to be loved, but they have enemies instead. Money makes enemies as well as friends.'

I noticed not for the first time that he spoke certain words ('American' was one) with something of a Yankee ring. 'You *are* English?' I asked.

'You can see my passport,' he said. 'Born in Brighton. You can't be more English than that.'

'It's only,' I apologized, for after all wasn't he trying to help me? 'that sometimes your accent . . .'

'An Atlantic accent,' he admitted. 'You see I spent years in the States learning my trade.'

'Trade?'

'Being a financial correspondent, so now here I am in a country with a hundred and twenty-three banks, and a socialist general in charge. It could turn a financial correspondent into a political correspondent – why, even a war correspondent – at the drop of a hat. It would be very useful then for my paper to have two neutrals reporting from here.'

'Why don't you recruit the Captain? He's had a lot of experience around the world.'

'What captain?'

'It's a name we always gave him – I mean my father.'

'Oh, he's busy enough – with his business – whatever it is. And his plane. Do you know by the way where he keeps his plane?'

'At the airport I suppose.'

'Yes, I suppose so. It was a silly question. I just never

happened to see it around. Of course there are two airports. The national and the international, and I generally find myself using the international.

'So you want me to ask him?'

'No, no, forget it. It was just idle curiosity. Well, to be truthful, not altogether idle. In my trade it can always happen that I need a small plane. I can pay well – I mean of course my paper can pay well, and there are so few private planes to be found around here.'

'Have you asked him?'

'One day I shall if I really feel the need, and I'm pretty sure he would always be ready to help me. After all he's a fellow Englishman, and in these parts I would rather trust an Englishman than a Yankee.'

'Why? If you are working for them.'

'Oh I don't mean the fellows on my paper, but journalism isn't a simple business in these parts. A good story can sometimes be a bit dangerous. There are people who mightn't want it published so that in a way it's comforting to have another Englishman . . .'

Our conversation 'in a way' seemed to be moving in circles and I found that, for some reason, I didn't believe a word that he was saying. I think Mr Quigly spotted my mistrust. He said, 'Here I am talking a lot of nonsense to you instead of going about my proper business. I have a lot to do today.'

'And what today is your business?'

'A story of course, it's always a story. If you don't have a new story for them nearly every week they feel you are not worth paying. Sometimes I must admit that it's as well to invent one.'

I could well understand his reasoning, for wasn't it the

way I had obtained my first job? Perhaps this was the first time I felt the possibility of a certain companionship with Mr Quigly. I would have liked, if he had been more specific, to help him. I took a step towards the desk to leave my key and I heard his voice behind me, 'Well, I'll be off. See you again soon,' but when I turned he was already gone, vanished, though not into thin air, for the air of Panama was damp and broody with the daily rain to come.

(7)

'I've something to show you,' the Captain told me. He had cut himself shaving and he leant close to the mirror in order to examine the wound. I was reminded of that occasion years ago when he had slit himself open in removing a beard.

'You should have kept that old beard of yours,' I said, 'then you wouldn't need to shave now.'

'That was years and years ago and anyway Liza didn't like the beard. When I came back, she told me I looked a different man, a man she didn't know.'

'I don't think it was the beard she minded.'

'I think you are right. But I'm surprised you noticed at that age.'

'She was afraid the police would catch you without it. If you shaved.'

'Right again. But things are very different now. I'm not dealing with the English coppers. They are used to simple things like a murder or a jewel theft. The people here can't be deceived by a beard – or a haircut. I have to be a great deal more careful than that. Everything here is politics.'

The Captain turned away from the mirror and said, 'Thank God, I'm not in danger of prison here. I'm only in danger of death.'

'Good heavens, why?'

'What on earth is there to worry about in death? Death is unavoidable anyway, so why should I care? And if all goes well, when I go at last, I'll leave Liza a rich woman.'

'She never wanted to be rich.'

'Oh, cut out that word rich. I want her to be secure, that's all – if something happens to me.'

My heart sank whenever he spoke of Liza, for he would have to learn some day that she was dead. Once again I regretted not telling him of her death at the start.

'I'm playing for higher stakes here,' he continued between strokes of the razor, 'than the odd thousand pounds of jewels, so of course the penalties are a lot higher. At least for those who think that death's a higher penalty than prison. But I know what a prison is like. I had enough of one in the war. Damn it, I've cut myself again. Give me my hemo stick. Why, I'd never have got out of that German prison camp if I had thought a prison better than death.'

'So that story's true?' I asked.

'Of course it's true. Why?'

'My father thought a lot of your stories were lies.'

'Oh it was the Devil who liked to lie, not me. And I did win you at backgammon not chess.'

'And all that story of escaping across the Pyrenees and the Spanish monks?'

'How else could I have taught you the bit of Spanish

you know, and how would I have got on here without it?'

'And all those mules?'

'Today,' he said, and he turned solemnly away from the mirror, lifting his razor much as a priest lifts the Host, 'I'm going to show you one of the mules in its own stable. You and I will be the only ones who know where the stable is — except of course a few of my real friends who will never, I hope, betray me.' He wiped the razor clean and faced me again. 'It's a big secret,' he said. 'You *are* one of my real friends, aren't you?'

Could I be blamed for giving him the answer, 'Yes, of course,' for if he was not my friend, who, literally on earth, was my friend now that Liza was dead?

(8)

We took the Captain's car — a not very expensive Renault — and drove away from the city, out beyond the banks and the slums — unchecked into the American Zone, past all the golfers and the barracks and the churches — the Captain named a few of the churches as we went by them — the Coco Solo Community Church, the Cross Roads Bible Church, the Nazarene, the Latter Day Saints, the Four Square Gospel — 'more than sixty of them,' he told me confirming Pablo's mathematics, 'though not so many as the banks.'

'Coco Solo,' I protested, thinking of Coca-Cola, 'you must have invented that.'

'Not invented, but perhaps I pointed to the wrong building. It may have been the Jehovah Witnesses or the

First Isthian. A very religious people, the Yankees. I forgot to show you the Argosy Book Stall. That is really unique. The only bookshop in the Zone. Of course with so much religion, not to speak of military duties, they have very little time to read.'

We drove left out of the Zone just as unchecked as we had gone in and then turned – I was going to write north, but points of the compass in Panama can be confusing even to a geographer. Who for example would guess that the Canal runs from the Atlantic to the Pacific more or less west to east? All I can remember now of our drive was a great hoarding by the road we took which exhibited the plan of a town to be built apparently one day by the Bank of Boston and not yet begun. There were only a number of light standards along cemented roads which led nowhere except to a huddle of huts on the edge of the Pacific.

'Here,' the Captain said, 'we turn right – and I would like you to forget where we are,' he added quickly as he bumped the car over a ditch and into a mass of grass and bushes shoulder high. We came out from them into a short runway which even to my amateur eye looked the worse for long wear.

'There she is,' the Captain proclaimed with an unmistakable note of pride as he stopped the car and pointed at a small plane parked on the rough ground.

'She looks a bit old,' I remarked.

'Thirteen years, but she's safe enough. If only they let her alone.' He was silent for quite a while and I thought that perhaps he was brooding on 'they', whoever 'they' were, but I was wrong. He broke the silence. 'You mustn't mention her when you write to her.'

I felt entangled by all the 'theys' and 'hers'. I asked, 'Mention who?'

'The plane of course. She'd be worried.'

Can a plane worry? I thought.

He sat a while silent at the wheel and I was afraid to break the silence, and silence in my situation was safer than words.

At last he spoke. 'She'll be all right.'

'The doctor said . . .' I began, but then I realized that this time it was the plane he meant, not Liza. Luckily it seemed that he hadn't caught my words, those dangerous words which might have opened the door and let the truth in. He said, 'I check her after every flight. It's not that I'm afraid of anything wrong, but I can't afford to let the others down.'

'The others?'

He didn't hear me, for his mind had already switched in another direction. 'You've written to her and told her you're here – safe?'

'Oh yes, I've written,' I said, for obviously this time he wasn't talking about the plane.

'When did you learn to fly?' I asked him.

'It was when I got back to England. I was fed up with the bloody infantry, but then the war came to an end just as I was passing my tests. I did no real flying. I never thought it would be of use until I came here. But in these parts I found I wanted a plane.'

'What for?'

'To be of real use to my friends. They needed a plane. To carry things which they badly want where you can't go by road. Would you like a spin?'

Looking at the thirteen-year-old second-hand plane I

would have dearly liked to say 'No', but I hadn't the courage and I nodded instead.

As we approached the plane it seemed, at every step I took, to become older and more fragile. There could have been at most room for three apart from the pilot, but as we came close to it the Captain paused and took a step back. He was gazing at the plane with reverence as though it were some sacred object which might grant his prayers, or as a man might look at a woman who has aged by his side but still holds his admiration by the way she has skilfully dealt with time. He said, 'Do you know what I would have liked to do for her?'

'No. What?'

'I would have liked to paint her wings just like they paint the buses here. You've seen them go by in the street with their coloured landscapes, even with madonnas you could pray to. Not that I'm a believer, but think how pretty she would look.'

'Why don't you paint her then?'

'Oh, it would never do. She'd be too identifiable. Perhaps one day I might when I retire from all this and don't use her for work any more. I can just see Liza sitting up there in the pilot's seat looking out at the painted trees on the wings or standing beside us down here, saying a prayer for us to the Madonna. There would be a landscape on one wing and a madonna on the other.'

'You say retire – retire from what?' But to that question he gave me no answer.

'We might have one spin together just for the fun of it,' he said. 'There's no one around to see us take off,' and in spite of my fears we did take off after many bumps.

I shall remember our flight very clearly – far more clearly than the events I have recorded earlier, which are often flawed by their touches of imagination. Over the forest of Darién we went in silence, with the deep green carpet unbroken below, without so much as a small tear in the surface. Once he nodded his head – east? west? south? impossible to say in the confused geography of Panama – and he remarked, 'Over there you can see Colombia. Where all this began,' but I had no idea of what he intended by 'all this'.

We reached the Atlantic and then we turned and dropped low over a small village by the sea. 'Nombre de Dios,' the Captain told me. I could see one old cannon lying in the grass and a scurry of retreating villagers who must have been unused to planes, for only a helicopter could have landed there.

'Where Drake's buried,' I said.

'No. His body's off Portobello further up.'

'But there was a poem I learnt at school. "Slung atween the round shot in Nombre de Dios Bay."'

'Poets never get things right. Drake's buried deep down in the water off Portobello, near where the Spaniards stored their gold.'

We headed back then towards the Pacific and for a long while not a single word was said. I wondered where his thoughts might be wandering, but as we began our descent I learnt at least something of the route they had taken, and it was to me a very dangerous one.

We were in sight of the ruins when he spoke first. 'I'm anxious about Liza. There should have been another letter.'

'The post to Panama is very slow.'

'Not that slow. Sometimes two weeks perhaps. If anything went wrong do they have my address?'

I hesitated. 'Who do you mean by they?'

'The doctors of course, the nurses.'

We were passing over the great Bridge of the Americas and a huddle of ships were waiting to enter the Canal. 'Yes,' I told him. 'They have it.' Apt something or other I thought, for I could no longer remember the number.

I felt I was drawing perilously near the end of the road of lies which I had been so recklessly treading. I said, 'I'll telegraph a friend to inquire if you like.'

'Yes, do that.'

The trouble was that I had no friend who knew enough to aid me in my deceit. It even occurred to me that I might ask aid of Mr Quigly. It was for more time that I was fighting, time to free myself somehow from my dependence on the Captain.

The plane was bumping over the rough turf of its hideout before he spoke again. 'Do it quickly. Do it as soon as you get to the hotel.'

'I'll go straight to the post office.'

'No need for that. There are always queues there. Send it from the hotel.'

My fury mounted – fury at my own cowardice. Anger muttered in my stomach all the way to the hotel in the way a kettle on a gas ring mutters as it approaches the boiling point. I felt I wasn't trusted and that infuriated me all the more because I knew very well that I wasn't trustworthy. Why should I be? I defended myself. Did a man who had been wanted so often by the police at home for his misdeeds and was now engaged in God knows what criminal enterprise in this strange little country of banks and poverty deserve any trust himself?

At the hotel he led me to the counter and commanded a telegraph form and then stood over me as I attempted to compose. I felt I could trust the English post office not to return an undelivered telegram all the way to Panama, but what name to put on it? All the Captain's aliases came first to my mind and blocked the imagination: Victor, Carver, Cardigan, Smith . . .

The Captain was impatient. 'Surely you know someone? Have you no friends in London?'

'Browne,' I wrote, as I remembered his own original name, and Browne with an e seemed to make the name more plausible. I added the number and street where I had my studio rooms. The message asked 'Browne' to call at the hospital and send news of Liza's health to me at the hotel. The Captain was still looking over my shoulder and I asked with undisguised iritation, 'Won't that do?'

'Yes, I suppose so. It could be a bit more glabrous.' That word bore for him a large variety of meanings which were unknown to me.

We went upstairs to the inevitable evening ceremony when the miniature whisky bottles were drawn from the hotel refrigerator.

'I have to finish my letter to Liza,' he told me, and with the taste of whisky my prudence left me for a moment.

'I hope that she will be able to read it,' I replied, thinking how to explain the lack of letters.

His hand shook so that he upset his glass. 'What on earth do you mean? You said it was a small accident.'

'Yes, yes, it seemed small.'

'What do you mean *seemed*?' I tried to right myself. 'Well, you know the shock. At a certain age . . .'

'She's not old,' he said with a note of ferocity, and of course I realized that to him, at *his* years, old age did not start till well after his own, and besides all the years of separation probably had no existence for him.

'No, no, that was not what I meant.'

But the anger rose in me. After all I was not only protecting myself, I was protecting *him* from the truth, but if he wanted the truth . . .

He said, 'You shouldn't have left Liza there alone if she's worse than you told me.'

'She wanted me to come. She asked me to come.'

'She was thinking of me. She never thinks of herself. You shouldn't have come.'

'If you don't want me here . . .' I had no idea of how to finish the sentence, but he finished it for me.

'You must go back. At once. Tomorrow I'll get you your ticket. There's a plane the day after.'

'And if I don't want to go?'

'I'm not going to give you a penny if you stay. Your place is with Liza.'

'I don't need your money. I've been offered a job.'

'A job!' he exclaimed with incredulity as though I had said, 'a fortune'. 'Who by?'

'A friend of yours.'

'You don't know any friends of mine.'

'By Mr Quigly.'

'Quigly! Don't you dare . . .'

He took a step towards me and I thought he was preparing to strike me. I backed towards the door and threw the truth at him like a glass of vitriol. 'There's no one to go back to. Liza's dead.'

(9)

I didn't wait to see his stricken face. I had no wish to pity the man, and so I made quickly for the stairs, not even waiting for the lift in case he followed me. I was afraid of him, but I felt no guilt at all as I scrambled down four flights and I was happy to find a lift door open on the eighth floor. All that he had done for me, save for that one far-off day at school, he had done only for the sake of Liza. I had no obligation to him. I had lied in order to win my independence, but how many lies had he told to win his, if indeed he was independent now?

In the hall I seized the telephone and for the first time I called the number which Mr Quigly had given me, but it was a strange voice that answered me with a genuine Yankee twang.

'Is Mr Quigly there?'

'Who's speakin'?'

'Smith – Jim Smith.'

There was a pause and then the same voice came back, an unfriendly voice I thought it; it was as though I had interrupted an intimate conversation. 'He says he'll ring you in the morning.'

I implored, 'If he's there, can't I speak to him, please? Tell him it's urgent.'

There was another long pause and then it was Mr Quigly who replied. 'What is it, Mr Smith?'

'It's not Mr Smith. It's Jim.'

'Jim?'

'His son.' The complexity of our relations increased at every moment.

'Oh, it's you.'

'Yes, it's me.'

'What's so urgent?'

'I can't tell you over the telephone. Can I come and see you? But I haven't your address.'

'It's difficult for me to see you here. Look. Wait a moment while I think. Come to that restaurant in a quarter of an hour. The one with the Pisco Sours. We can talk alone there.'

I put down the telephone and went out into the night, uncertain of my route and of my future. The banks stood around me like immense tombstones, lit only on the lowest floors by the light from the little houses of the rich which lay among them. I took several wrong turnings, afraid always of finding myself suddenly in that other Panama, of dirt and penury and drugs, or that by crossing a street I might enter a different country altogether, the United States of America. Nor did I remember the name of the restaurant. There were few taxis about and no ranks, and it was only by repeating the words 'restaurant' and 'Peru' to several passers-by that I came on the rendezvous at last.

Mr Quigly had not yet arrived. I bought myself a Pisco Sour out of what remained of the money Liza had given me and waited with impatience and apprehension. The restaurant was nearly empty and there were very few people in the streets where Pablo had warned me that muggings were frequent at night. Although I sipped it slowly my Sour was finished long before a taxi drew up and Mr Quigly appeared in the doorway. The Sour had not mixed well with the whisky in my stomach, and Mr Quigly in my eyes looked more narrow than he had ever done before.

'I'm sorry I was a little delayed,' he apologized. 'In my line of business the unexpected is always liable to happen.' He seemed to choose his words with the slow care of a leader writer for a paper of quality. 'I see you have had a Pisco Sour. Can I offer you another?'

'It was a mistake,' I said. 'It doesn't go with whisky.'

'Another whisky then. And perhaps I'll take one myself. For me it has been a long dry evening.'

I told him, 'No I won't take anything. I want to tell you that I've quarrelled finally with the Captain.'

'The Captain?'

'The man you call Smith.'

Mr Quigly didn't answer for a while. He seemed to be plunged in reflection, and when he answered it was in a tone of reproach. 'Was that really necessary?'

'He's giving me my ticket home. He wants me to go on the first possible plane.'

'And you?'

'I don't want to go. I told him you had offered me a job.'

'And what did he say to that?'

'He was furious. I was afraid of him. I went away.'

Mr Quigly again seemed sunk in thought. He was not an impulsive man I knew by this time. Perhaps he was calculating in figures as he had at the airport, not ten but twelve. At last he spoke again. 'I must say I find myself a little at sea. Why was he so angry? You seemed to have talked a little rashly about that job. Nothing is quite settled yet. After all he's your father. He has a right . . .'

'But he isn't my father. He won me at backgammon – or at chess. The Devil says it was chess.'

'Who on earth is the Devil?'

'My real father.'

'Oh dear, oh dear,' Mr Quigly said. 'I think before we settle about a job you'll have to make things a little clearer to me. I haven't the final word you know. There are others I have to persuade.'

So I told him as briefly as I could the story of myself and Liza and our life with the Captain and his frequent disappearances and changes of name. I told him too of Liza's death and how I had lied to the Captain.

He surprised me by his comment when I had finished. 'Why, it's quite a love story.'

'I don't know about the love,' I said.

'Well, at least they seemed to have – how shall I put it – needed each other. I suppose that could be called love.' Mr Quigly spoke like one who had as little experience in that domain as I had and depended on hearsay. 'What do you suppose he did to keep you both? A single man who takes on a family. It's no light thing.'

'We never knew exactly what he did, but the police seemed always interested in him.'

'I too have often wondered,' Mr Quigly said. 'He seems to earn a lot of money here with that plane of his. Charter flights I suppose. But carrying what? Well, I think I know the answer to that. And how did he get a plane in the first place?'

'He told me it all began in Colombia.'

'Yes, I did get to know something of that from a

colleague of mine in Caracas. Probably drugs. Nothing very serious I should imagine. Not hard drugs. Just marijuana. Baby stuff. He dropped the traffic pretty soon I imagine and flew here. Perhaps it was too dangerous or perhaps his conscience . . . Has he a conscience? Anyway I doubt if he ever paid for his plane because I happen to know – from my colleague – that one country he'll never go back to around here is Colombia. I think he may be wanted there by his old comrades.'

'You seem to know a lot. I thought you were only a financial correspondent.'

Mr Quigly gave his abrupt little giggle, a giggle which was as narrow as himself. There was no humour in it, or, if there was, it was a humour as tightly confining as his trousers.

'Finance,' he said, 'comes into everything. Politics, war, marriage, crime, adultery. Everything that exists in the world has something to do with money. Even religion. The priest has to buy his bread and wine and the criminal has to buy his gun – or his plane.'

'But you think the drug business is over?'

'I am sure of it. He wouldn't be protected by Colonel Martínez in the drug business, and he *is* protected.'

'Who is this Colonel Martínez?'

'Well, it's difficult to say exactly. An important officer in the National Guard.'

'Are you protected?'

'They don't exactly protect me so far as I can tell, but of course they are interested in me. You see, I work for an American paper . . . they're apt to be suspicious of anything American.'

'What use is an old plane like the Captain's?'

'Oh, he can't carry very heavy stuff of course, but it's not the heavy stuff which the guerrillas need.'

'Guerrillas? In Panama?'

'No, no, not in Panama, but you know the phrase "The enemy of my enemy is my friend." The people here hate the Zone. In Nicaragua they are fighting Somoza and in Salvador they are fighting the death squads – and both Somoza and the death squads are helped by the United States.'

'And where are you in all this?'

'I've told you. I'm only a financial correspondent. My paper is not very important, but I'm pretty sure my information is read even in the *Wall Street Journal*. Of course I am English. I'm neutral, but news is news. Even news about the small stuff. You see, the small stuff has to be bought somewhere. Of course the Yankees say it comes from Russia or Cuba. Anyone who fights a dictator controlled by them is a Communist. It's a useful way of explaining things to the great public and perhaps they are right. It wouldn't do to say that their friend Israel might be ready to sell a few tanks to *their* friends the dictators. Finance you see, finance in everything. I am a financial correspondent and I need information.'

I was surprised by Mr Quigly. Behind all his evasions and abstractions he was for once remarkably frank.

'And you are ready to give me a job?' I challenged him.

'A small retainer I should say while I consult my editor. What about another whisky?'

I agreed, for whisky had certainly loosened Mr Quigly's tongue. He held this one in his hand without even sipping it. He gazed deep into the glass like a medium who is looking for an image in a crystal ball. At last – perhaps he had seen the image which he was seeking – he said, 'I regard your father, I mean Mr Smith, or what is it you call him, the Captain, as a friend whom I had hoped to know much better. In helping you I thought that I might be indirectly helping him. We can help each other in little ways. I am really rather distressed to hear that you have quarrelled with him.' He added with unexpected crudity, 'After all he's in it for the money as much as I am, and we might easily have come to work together. It's all a financial affair when you come down to it. My friends could pay him a lot better than the guerrillas. Have you seen his plane?'

'He's taken me for a ride.'

'I've always wondered where he kept it. Perhaps you could give me a clue.'

I was still lost – I don't think it was only the whisky which bemused me. I said, 'The clue I want is where to spend the night. I suppose there are cheap hotels even in Panama.'

'I would not advise a cheap hotel in Panama. But you don't need to worry. To tell you the truth it's Mr Smith I have to worry about. He can be rash. I'd like to see your father – sorry, Mr Smith – and try to make up for this unnecessary quarrel. Perhaps he's flown off in a rage. If he's not at the hotel. Where do you say he kept his plane?'

I had said nothing, but now I told him as best I could. It was the map of the unmade town which caught his attention. 'Oh there, how very odd. What possible shelter?'

'Oh, there's a sort of hut.'

The drinks had loosened my tongue too and freed my curiosity. 'What I don't understand is how you two could possibly work together. You haven't told me anything clearly, but I can tell you are on opposite sides.'

'There are no opposite sides where money is concerned. He's not working for a cause. He's working for that adopted mother of yours and now she's dead. He doesn't need money for her any longer. He doesn't need money for you. I can find you all you need. He needs a little for himself of course, and I can help him there, if only he would listen to me.'

'How?'

'I'll pay him well for any information he can give me.'

I noticed Mr Quigly always used the word information, never intelligence. Perhaps he thought it a more innocuous word.

'Do you agree,' Mr Quigly asked, 'that I go and see him first thing in the morning? He will have had time to think things over. The changed situation. Your mother's – what's her name? – Liza's death.'

'You can do what you like. It won't do you any good. He'll never forgive me for my lies.'

'Perhaps I can show them to him from a new angle.'

'He doesn't trust you.'

'Perhaps not me. But in finance one trusts one's bank. I could be his bank.'

I was tired of the two words, bank and finance. I wanted to sleep.

Mr Quigly in the end was very obliging. He found me a room of a sort not very far off and paid for the night's rent in advance. Before he left he asked me to call him Fred. 'My name is Cyril,' he said, 'but all my real friends call me Fred.' It was as if he was putting his signature – true or false – to an agreement, and I couldn't help feeling that Cyril suited him far better than the colloquial Fred.

(10)

I was woken around ten and fetched to the telephone. A voice said, 'Fred speaking,' and for a long moment I couldn't remember who Fred was. 'Quigly,' the voice explained with impatience. 'I'm at the Continental Hotel. Please come at once.'

'I can't come at once. I'm not dressed.'

'Then dress quickly, please.' He spoke almost as though he were already my employer.

I found him waiting in the lobby and he drew me away out of earshot of the porter.

'He's gone,' he said.

'Gone where?'

'It's what I'd like to know. The porter's got a letter for him. With an English stamp. That's interesting. Ask him to give it to you. Say you are off to see him. And ask him to give you back the key of his room. They won't let *me* have it, but they know you shared it and it's still reserved.'

'Why should I want the key back – or you?'

'There may be indications.'

'Of what?'

'Of what he's up to.'

'I thought you knew – something to do with arms.'

'As a newspaper man,' he was still clinging to that unlikely cover, 'I want details.'

(161)

'If they are financial, I suppose,' I said to mock him, 'they will interest the *Wall Street Journal*.'

But he was quite unconscious of my teasing. 'Yes, his finances are of great interest, and who finances him. I think this letter may give us a clue.'

I gave way to him and went to fetch the letter and the key. There was no difficulty. The porter probably thought I had spent the night there. Up in the room we had shared Mr Quigly moved quickly around. 'He can't be gone far,' he said. 'He's coming back tonight.' And he held up a pair of pyjamas lying on the sofa unfolded.

I said, 'I used the sofa. Those are my pyjamas.'

'Ah,' he wasn't disappointed, for he had turned over a pillow on the bed, 'then these are his. So it comes to the same thing. He expects to return.'

'Are you glad of that?'

'Yes, for it's much easier to keep an eye on him here. I expect that he'll be going by his usual route. Over Costa Rica. Then across the border to drop the arms somewhere in the Estelí region where the Sandinistas are strongest.'

'I don't even know what country you are talking about.'

'Look in the wardrobe, while I go through the waste-paper basket.'

I obeyed him. I was beginning to be interested myself. I had never followed as closely as we were doing now the Captain's activities, which had kept Liza and myself in a kind of demi-comfort through so many years. The nearest I had ever come to what Mr Quigly liked to call 'information' was that line I had read in the *Telegraph* about a man 'with a military bearing' who had asked the way at the jeweller's shop to 'Baxter Street'. Baxter Street and Estelí – two unknown places cropping up with so many years between them.

'Where's Estelí?' I asked.

'I told you. Where Somoza's National Guard is weakest and the Sandinistas strongest.'

'What country are you talking about?'

'You seem an ignorant sort of fellow. Don't you know that there's a civil war in Nicaragua? At least lend me a hand and look at the wardrobe.'

'Nothing there. Only a suit and some shirts.'

'Anything in the pockets?'

'Nothing,' I lied, for there was indeed a letter which I had slipped into one of my own pockets without looking at the address. I was not yet an employee of Mr Quigly I told myself. A room for one night without even a meagre breakfast was not a binding obligation.

'He's obviously planning to return,' Mr Quigly said, 'but perhaps we could still intercept him before he leaves. They say he only went away half an hour ago. He won't have got far in that old Renault of his and it won't hold much of an arsenal. Probably a few grenades. Not that they're much good against Somoza's tanks, US supplied. Don't despise financial information. It's wonderfully intricate. That English stamp. You say that his woman's dead, so who's his correspondent? Never mind now. We've got to move quick. If we can catch him with anti-tank grenades in the plane I don't see how Colonel Martínez could cover him up without a scandal. And a scandal would suit the Yankees well enough – as well as my paper of course. Any paper loves a scandal.'

'But where do you want to go?'

'To his plane of course. You know where he keeps it.'

A disturbed hot night in a small hotel with a hard pillow and a window which wouldn't open had kept my anger against the Captain still alive, so I didn't hesitate. I would earn my bonus.

Mr Quigly's Mercedes for the first time impressed me. When he met me at the airport I had been too tired to take notice of it. I sat beside him and directed him a bit uncertainly – over the great bridge, past the military instalments of the Zone, the churches, the golf links, the smart villas, back into Panama, until we reached the map of the non-existent town. 'Go slow here,' I told him. 'There's a turning to take.'

He obeyed but his thoughts were elsewhere. He said, 'If we catch him the scandal might kill the Canal Treaty. The Senate would be happy.'

'What Canal treaty?'

He ignored my ignorance. 'And Congress too.' He added, 'That letter with the English stamp. You might read it to me while we drive.'

'I don't think he would like me to give him an envelope I'd opened.'

'I have a strong feeling we are too late. We may never see him again. All right. Have it your way. Keep the letter closed until we reach – what do you call it? his runway. Or should we say his runaway. If he's not there I see no reason why you shouldn't open it. Even if he returns he'll never know there was a letter.'

'It wouldn't interest you. I know the writing on the envelope. It's from a dead woman.'

'A dead woman?'

'Liza.'

'Ah well, forget it. He knows how long letters take to reach Panama.'

'Stop here. I'm almost sure it's the place.'

I looked at the bushes and saw the trampled signs of the Renault's passing. We followed bumping on its track until I saw the runway and the empty shed.

'My goodness,' Mr Quigly exclaimed (I was never to hear him use a stronger expletive). 'It's a bit rough, isn't it? I wouldn't like to come down here – or take off, with a load of anti-tank missiles too perhaps.'

He sat staring for a while, then he turned on his engine. 'I must get back and send a telegram.'

'Financial information?'

'You wouldn't be far wrong to call it that,' he replied with his usual caution.

He drove me back in a glum and broody silence while I wondered if he used some kind of code in his telegrams – perhaps something as simple as the book code which as a boy I had once read about in a novel of espionage. The spy and his correspondents chose a sentence out of an agreed book, perhaps an edition of the complete works of Shakespeare, which would give a wide choice of lines to play with, and on that sentence and its order of words the code was somehow based. I tried to imagine what kind of book Mr Quigly and his Americans would have chosen. Not Updike. Updike was too short for safety. Perhaps he would have gone back to some long classic like *Gone With The Wind*.

At the Continental Mr Quigly broke his silence. 'No point,' he said, 'in being uncomfortable. The room you shared is still reserved. You could even use the bed. I'll telephone you at once when I have news of him.'

I collected the key from the porter who told me, 'There's a telephone message for your father,' and I read it in the lift. 'Please telephone the office of Colonel Martínez.' Well, I thought, Colonel Martínez would have to wait a long while for a reply.

The two unread letters in my pocket weighed on my mind, and as soon as I was alone I opened first the one which was addressed legitimately to me. A cheque and a ticket came out first and then the letter. It amazed me by its length, and as I read by its contents. Something after all the years of discretion had made him speak at last, and that something of course was the death of Liza.

Jim, you have been lying to me every day since you arrived and God alone knows why you didn't continue. I suppose you were waiting till I found you a job and set you up to live on me as you have lived on me all these years. I kept you for Liza's sake, but Liza is dead. I don't want to see your face again – it bears too many memories of Liza. Here's your ticket home to London and a cheque which will keep you for a few weeks if you cash it here before you go, time for you to get a job at home. You've no place here. But my last advice to you and my last responsibility to you is to warn you to keep clear of that man Quigly. I'm sorry I ever asked his help to meet you, but he was around and he's always ready to do small things for me. It's his way of keeping in touch with me, and he's paid for that by his employers and God damn them all. They never got a penny's worth of value out of me.

You've no reason at all to trust me. I know that well. I've been a liar too, but I've never lied to you or, whatever the old Devil may have told you, to Liza – only to the coppers. It's a fuliginous story, I know that. When I began I didn't steal to make myself rich. I stole without an object. It was a game, a risky game like roulette. In war one begins to enjoy a little danger. In that German camp I was bored to death by safety and when I got over the frontier I was bored by the peace of the Spanish monastery. Back in England learning to fly was only too easy like getting a car licence. Then peace came almost as soon I got into the air. No danger. No glabrous excitement. So I stole. That was amusement enough until I met the Devil and saw poor Liza in the hospital and the child she wanted so much was killed inside her by order of the Devil. I don't know that she ever really cared much for me. She was an honest girl and I don't think she would ever have liked to use the word love untruly. Since then I've played the danger game only for her sake so that one day she might be safe when I was gone. When you told me she was dead, I knew that I wasn't needed by her any more. I never took risks, serious risks, after I met Liza, but now all my responsibility is over. Thank God, if he should exist, for granting me that at least. I'm not unhappy, nothing bad can happen to Liza any longer, she's free and I'm free at last, and free of you too. I've escaped from the prison camp again. There's one useful thing I can do for my friends now that Liza's gone, and I can take any risk I like. For you I've done enough. I don't want you to write to me. I won't read anything you write. You've betrayed Liza. Don't wait for me when you get this letter. Go away and never come back.

He signed the letter, 'The Captain, the Colonel, the Major, the Sergeant, Señor Smith' with an exclamation mark after each name. I wondered why he hadn't added his real name, but I suppose he wanted to preserve one at least of his names out of use. After all he and I had never been much closer than strangers since that gin and tonic of his and the lunch of smoked salmon. All his interest had lain in Liza, and there ironically was her letter which had arrived too late for him to read and which might have broken the news of her death more gently than I had done. I was sorry for that, and yet I found his letter hard to digest.

I opened the letter which he would never now read. Liza was not given to writing long letters and this was very short. She wrote, 'Dear Captain, I know what the doctor and the nurse are trying not to tell me, that I shall soon be dead. So now I'm writing what I've always been too shy to say. I've loved you ever since the day you came to see me with the Devil in hospital. You had lost a button off your shirt and your shoes could have done with a good clean. You were the kindest man I've ever known. Liza.'

The letter astonished me. So there had been, after all, some kind of love between them. Whatever that phrase meant it seemed more durable than the casual sexual interludes which I had in my way enjoyed. As I lay on the sofa in the Captain's room awaiting sleep which was long in coming, I felt a stab of jealous pain. To have remembered that missing button through all the years of unexplained absences, this was something beyond my imagination, and I was seized with a furious sense of inferiority. I was shut out, an Amalekite again. All the same I kept the letter. It might please him and soften his anger if he came back, but as I dozed into sleep I was angry with both of them and all the inexplicable world which they represented. I had an odd dream of walking down a long rough road towards a deep and dark wood which retreated as I advanced. I had for some reason to penetrate that wood, but I became more and more exhausted until I was woken by the crying of the telephone beside the Captain's bed. I was reluctant to pick up the receiver. I feared that I would hear the Captain's voice, but it was Mr Quigly's.

'Is that Jim?'

'Yes.'

'I've been ringing a long time. Four and a half minutes.' Always that precision in the way of figures. Perhaps it was the quality of the financial profession.

'I was asleep.'

'I've been rung up by Colonel Martínez. He's never rung me before. It must be important. He wants to see you. He had sent to that place I put you in, but you weren't there. Are you listening?'

'Yes. How did he know where I slept?'

'Ask him. It's his job to know. Pablo is on the way to fetch you. Don't tell him anything.'

'Pablo?'

'No, no. Colonel Martínez, of course.'

There was a knock on the door and I put down the receiver. I'd had enough of Mr Quigly. I opened the door and Pablo was there.

There seemed to be a sentry everywhere to whom Pablo had to show his pass – at the gates of the National Guard headquarters, at the doorway of the building we entered, outside the waiting-room to which we were ushered. Pablo said not a word and sat beside me in silence. His revolver pressed uncomfortably against my hip and I became impatient. 'Colonel Martínez,' I said, 'seems to be a busy man,' but Pablo made no reply.

When my turn came at last Pablo left me at the door, and I looked across the room at the Colonel with curiosity. No policeman would ever have described him as a man with a military bearing. He had a kindly, pale and anxious face and when he stood up to greet me I could see that he was short and a little tubby.

'I am sorry to have kept you waiting, Mr Smith,' he said, speaking English slowly and with care, and yet with that Yankee twang which living a lifetime close alongside the American Zone had perhaps produced.

'Baxter,' I corrected him and he looked down and shuffled some papers on his desk and corrected himself, 'Mr Baxter'. Then there was a long pause. Had he forgotten the purpose of my being there just as he had forgotten my true name? Anyway I knew that I liked him a good deal better than Mr Quigly. There was an innocence about him which I wouldn't have associated with a military uniform – or a policeman's.

He said, 'Do sit down, Mr Baxter. We are a little worried about Mr Smith – his unexpected absence. He was to have done a small job for us, but he seems to have disappeared into the blue.' He was troubled by a little cough which conveniently covered my silence. 'Of course we know you are a friend of Mr Quigly' – the word 'we' as he used it seemed to cover the whole of the National Guard, and for a moment I was surprised at the trouble they had taken to notice an insignificant stranger, until I remembered Pablo. Of course he would have reported. I said, 'Not really a friend.'

The Colonel said, 'Mr Quigly is an excellent journalist and working as he does for a gringo paper he has sources of information closed to us. We wondered if perhaps he had said a word to you which might indicate . . . We are anxious to have news of Mr Smith.'

I thought of the letter, but I obeyed Mr Quigly's instruction. 'I have none,' I said.

'Both of you were seen calling at the Continental Hotel yesterday morning and we supposed that you were trying to see your father. We thought perhaps he might have told you something . . .'

I ignored the small flaw in their information about my relations with the Captain and I said, 'Not a word. He wasn't there. He'd gone.'

'Yes, yes, gone, we know, and his plane too. But I thought that earlier than that he might have given you some indication . . . I assure you that we are worried – worried for his safety, Mr Baxter.' With his eyes bent over his papers he said in a low voice as though he were ashamed at having to give away a valuable piece of information: 'He was seen flying off, but he took the wrong direction.'

'The wrong direction?'

'Not the direction which he had been ordered to take.' There was a long pause as Colonel Martínez stared down at his papers. I thought: has he too taken a wrong direction?

The doubts in my mind harassed me and I tried to resolve them, with what seemed even to my own ears in this hushed room a question vulgarly direct. 'Who gave him the order? You or Mr Quigly?'

Colonel Martínez looked up at me and gave a little sigh like someone who has been relieved from a burden of discretion. 'Ah yes, Mr Quigly! What exactly do you know of Mr Quigly?'

'I know that he has offered me a job.'

'Are you going to take it?'

'Mr Smith has left me a letter with a cheque. He wants me to go home immediately.'

'And you are going?'

'I want to tell him first what I plan.'

Colonel Martínez said, 'I can only hope for all our sakes that will prove possible.'

I was completely at a loss. I told him, 'I don't know what you mean. Has he done something wrong? Is he in prison?'

'Certainly not. He is our friend. We put a great value on all the work he has done for us. We have need of him.' That damned word 'need' again.

'And how does Mr Quigly come into all this?'

'Well, I wouldn't describe Mr Quigly as his friend.'

'But' – the name always made me hesitate – 'Mr Smith sent Mr Quigly to meet me when I arrived.'

'Oh, we were very content that Mr Smith should have a certain contact with Mr Quigly. We say nothing against Mr Quigly. If you decide to work for Mr Quigly it's your decision, but perhaps if that happens we could give you a little advice. The advice I would give you now is just to wait. Don't make up your mind until – as we hope will happen – you have spoken again to your father.'

He patted the papers on his desk and rose with a friendly smile to show that the interview – interrogation? – was at an end. He said, 'Of course we shall let you know as soon as we have news of your father.'

(12)

But it was not Colonel Martínez who gave me the first news. It was Mr Quigly two hours later, or, as he would certainly have put it himself, two hours twelve minutes later. I had returned to the Captain's room in the hotel, for I had nowhere else to go. I lay on the sofa, but I couldn't sleep. All that was left for me to pass the time was thought – and *how* I thought, how I turned things over in my worried and twisted mind. It was as though I had been holding out my fist – as a child I had often done this for Liza – for a ball of knitting wool to be wound around it, and then I had carelessly moved and got the wool tangled.

Why were they anxious about the Captain's absence – an absence of only a few hours? Hadn't his life been full of absences since that first absence of his from the German prison camp was discovered by his guards if the story he told me was true? Did Mr Quigly and the Colonel fear a betrayal, but wasn't his life full of betrayals? He had pretended to love Liza and yet he had left her continually for reasons which he never explained. Who was this Somoza of whom Colonel Martínez spoke and who were the Sandinistas? I was abysmally ignorant, I realized well enough, of all that might be happening in these unknown regions. My work as a journalist had been confined to a very small area of England. Once I had travelled on a story as far as Ipswich, on the track of an odd and rather comic tale about a thief. The Captain too was a thief. My mind shifted again back and forth and the wool became even more tangled. And Quigly? Who was Quigly? What was Quigly?

It was when I was asking myself these questions which were the most difficult of all to answer that the telephone rang. I knew at once what the voice at the other end would say (it would be the code word 'Fred') so I let it ring on and on. In a way the sound was a relief: the questions had stopped and the wool fell off my wrists.

At last the ringing ceased and after a short interval what I expected came: a knock on the door. I felt I had to open it and there, of course, was Mr Quigly.

'I was ringing from below. They told me you were up here. Why didn't you answer?'

'I was busy thinking, Mr Quigly. Or should I call you Fred?'

'This is no joke, Jim. I've had news, bad news. Your father, I'm sorry, I mean Mr Smith, he's dead.' It flashed through my mind that at least Mr Quigly hadn't played for time as I had done when the Captain spoke to me of Liza. I was grateful to him for that. It seemed in a strange way to clear the air. I had no need to pretend a sorrow which I didn't feel.

'Are you sure? Colonel Martínez said he would let me know about him.'

'Ah, but he probably hasn't heard himself yet. You see

Mr Smith took the wrong direction.' Those were the same words which Colonel Martínez had used to me.

'You mean if he had taken the right one . . .'

'Colonel Martínez would have known where he was and he would be alive.'

'What was the wrong direction?'

'A nearly suicidal one. He must have known it was unlikely he would come back. I expect he never wanted to come back. He only wanted to help his friends and die.'

'How would that help his friends?'

'Because he would have killed Somoza too.'

'Somoza?'

Would I ever cease to be a stranger in this region of the world where I was at a loss to remember all the names?

'Oh, President Somoza survived all right – to please *my* friends.'

So, I thought, now it is all over, our quarrel and his life.

Mr Quigly went on, 'He was in no danger from us. We wanted to keep him alive. If only to discover where exactly he was dumping his arms.'

'What do you all mean – the wrong direction? How did he die?'

'His plane crashed near the bunker in Managua where Somoza stays at night these days. The plane must have been as full as he could make it of explosives, but all he did was kill himself and break a few windows in the Intercontinental Hotel across the way. No one else was hurt – only himself.'

'Oh, *he* wasn't hurt,' I said. 'He's free of me and Liza and all the others.'

'The others?'

'All who needed him.'

'His death is a waste. He was even a little useful to us in his way. What will you do – Jim?' He hesitated over the Christian name.

'He's left me enough money to go home.'

'Will you go?'

'I haven't got a home.' It was not in self-pity that I used the phrase, it was a cold statement of fact. I was like a man without a passport, only a card of residence.

Mr Quigly said, 'I'm pretty sure that I can fix things for you if you will only stay. You know you have quite a bit of value, Jim.' He didn't hesitate this time over the name. 'After all he *was* your father, and perhaps through you we might be able to contact and speak to some of his old friends.'

'But he wasn't my father.'

'Oh, yes, I forgot, but we mustn't be too literal, Jim.'

'And Colonel Martínez?'

'I'm sure he'll be your friend too if you give him the chance. You don't need to take sides between us. That's something we shall have to talk about together. You can be of help to both of us. I'm sure that if you stay everything can be arranged satisfactorily.'

I felt lost in all his ambiguities. They were like a twisting country road with many signposts which had been long abandoned by heavy traffic. I found myself for a moment regretting the great auto routes and the thunder of heavy lorries. I said, 'Go away, Mr Quigly. I want to be alone.'

Mr Quigly hesitated. 'But we are friends, Jim. I came here as a friend.'

'Yes, yes,' I agreed without conviction in order to get

rid of him and he went. But before he left he dropped an envelope on the bed. 'Just in case you are running short,' he said and was gone again into the city of a hundred and twenty-three banks. I thought, as I opened his envelope, 'So here one obviously pays cash even for friendship.' I put the money in my pocket – five two hundred dollar bills, and heard the telephone ring again. This time it was Pablo. He said, 'Colonel Martínez wants to see you again. He has news for you.'

It amused me to tell him, 'He needn't trouble to see me. I have the news already. From Mr Quigly.'

There was a long silence on the line. I imagined Pablo in the Colonel's office passing on this piece of news and waiting for his reply. It came at last. 'Colonel Martínez says that it is important all the same that you should see him. At once. He is sending me with a car for you.'

(13)

While I wait for Pablo I am spending the time bringing this narrative to a close. With the Captain dead what is the point of continuing it? I realize more than ever that I am no writer. A real writer's ambition doesn't die with his main character.

What now? I have a return ticket to London (but I can turn that in) and the dollars left me by the Captain and Mr Quigly. Shall I take Mr Quigly's advice and enter a world of secrecy and danger which will lead me I don't know where. I don't blame myself. It is the Captain who is responsible. He knew where he was going when he stole the jewels, when he crashed his plane. Sometimes if I think of the Captain I imagine that in some strange way he will prove one day to have been my real father if only for this legacy of illegality which he has injected into my bloodstream. I remember again the dream I had last night before Mr Quigly woke me, with an added detail, which I had forgotten. All that remained in my mind when I woke was the dark path which I was following into some deep wood, but now the reason for my walk came back to me. I had been following two mules which stopped again and again to crop the grass. There was nothing on their backs and I had no idea why I was pursuing them. The Captain of course would have known. How often he had spoken to me of those mules, but in his version they always carried sacks of gold.

One can hate one's father and even though I may choose to follow in his footsteps, it will still be hate that I shall feel. Compared with Liza I was nothing to him. He looked after her till her death, but me – he has left me this unfeeling legacy of a ticket of return to a place I have left for ever and if I stay here one thing I know for sure. I shall write no more. The bell of my room is ringing. It's almost certainly Pablo, coming to take me to see Colonel Martínez, and afterwards what do I do? Shall I tell Mr Quigly what passed between me and the Colonel? Do I take Mr Quigly's money? Will the Colonel offer me money – or only advice? The Captain would have advised me from his own experience, but he's safe and dead, and anyway would I have trusted him? It was only for Liza that he cared if he ever cared for her. We have both been a burden to him. And then *King Kong* came back into my mind and the words he had used to me then when I watched the King with his burden – a burden which kicked him so hard that I wondered why he didn't drop her into the street below: 'He loves her, boy, can't you understand that?' Perhaps I have never understood the nature of love. Perhaps . . . I wish I had seen him once more or that I hadn't lied to him at the beginning.

(14)

When I returned to this room from seeing Colonel Martínez I found in the kitchen some torn scraps of paper in the waste-paper basket which both I and Mr Quigly had missed. He had probably assumed that anything of real importance would have been burnt or shredded. He was a professional.

I think these scraps may have formed part of the letter the Captain had left for me and perhaps he thought they told too much about his weakness. I stuck them together and put them down now as a conclusion to this failed book of mine which no one will ever publish or read.

What do *I* need? Why the hell is it that I am always the one who seems to be needed. There was an old woman in the street once in Manchester and I needed what little I had far more than she needed it, but I suppose it wasn't her fault that she couldn't feel my need, and I could feel hers. It's not natural though. If I had the strength of King Kong . . .

The last sentence became quite unreadable. Strange that he too had remembered King Kong.

Enough of all this nonsense. I have more than a thousand and ten dollars (I counted them like Mr Quigly) as well as the money the Captain left me and the ticket which I can trade in. I write a line under all this scroll before I throw the whole thing into the same waste-paper basket, where anyone who chooses can find it. The line means Finis. I'm on my own now and I am following my own mules to find my own future.

———————————————

PART
IV

9

Colonel Martínez looked with a hint of amusement in his eyes at Mr Quigly. He said, 'This time we got to Mr Smith's room before you. The parcel was found in the waste-paper basket. Did the young man really throw it away because he had no intention of writing any more? But then why didn't he destroy it? I doubt if we shall ever learn the real reason. He's on his way – somewhere. My translator has had no time to do more than deal with the last pages beginning with his arrival in Panama. When he meets you, it is then that his account becomes interesting. The boy seems to have had a certain talent and it's a pity he didn't stick to writing, for writing is a safe occupation. I wanted to see you because there are so many references to you in – shall I call it his novel, Señor Quigly?'

'Well, I was a friend of his father.'

'Not a very close friend we have reason to believe.'

'Well, quite often I was able to help him in small ways. Like when I met Jim at the airport.'

'And you got news of Señor Smith's death quicker than we did, so perhaps we haven't taken you seriously enough, Señor Quigly. Did you warn Somoza's people in Managua of the route he was taking?'

'How could I have known?'

'Yes. I wish I could answer that. How? Another question? Who was King Kong?'

'King Kong?'

'A code name perhaps?'

'I wouldn't know. We don't use codes on my newspaper.'

'And you have no news of course of where Jim is? I'm afraid he may well have imitated Mr Smith too closely.'

'I've only seen him once since his father died.'

'You are generally very scrupulous with numbers, Señor Quigly. Think again.'

Mr Quigly thought again. 'Well perhaps I should have said two or three times.'

'You offered him employment, didn't you?'

'Nothing was really settled. A stringer's job. He had very little experience.'

'I ask you again – who was King Kong?'

'Some sort of monkey I seem to remember.'

'A monkey?'

'Perhaps a gorilla – I don't really remember which.'

Colonel Martínez gave a little sigh which might have been one of despair. 'You have a British passport I believe, Señor Quigly?'

'Yes.'

'And an American visa?'

'Yes. I have to visit my paper from time to time in New York.'

'Of course you know that next month the Canal Treaty will be signed by President Carter and General Torrijos, and then most of the American Zone will be in our hands.'

'Your General has done a good job and I congratulate you.'

'It's important that no stupid problems should occur

before the Treaty has been signed in Washington. We have our enemies there. I'm sure you will understand that.'

'Of course.'

'All the same I do feel a certain responsibility. His so-called father . . . one might say, I suppose, that he was partly responsible if something has happened to the young man. But you and I have our share of responsibility too.'

'I'm responsible for nothing.'

'You probably paid his father on occasion and, as you must certainly know, I paid him too.'

'I wish you wouldn't keep on calling Mr Smith his father.'

'I'm sorry, we are both a little inexact. Mr Smith's real name of course was Brown.'

'Anyway what's the worry, Colonel? Jim's probably on his way back to London by now. He told me he might be going home. Smith left him a ticket.'

'Not much of a home it seems. Let's be frank with each other, Señor Quigly. You knew, didn't you, that Smith had taken what I called the wrong direction.'

'How could I possibly know?'

'I think you played a bit of comedy when you went to look for his plane. You had already warned the National Guard and Somoza. They shot him down before he reached the bunker. Why? They would have known the Sandinistas had no plane.'

'You are wrong there, Colonel. They would certainly have known about Smith's plane. He has been dumping arms up in the Estelí region for quite a while.'

'I wonder whether it was you who warned them of

that . . . Never mind. It's of little concern now, except . . .'

Colonel Martínez stared down at the pile of manuscript on his desk. He said, 'I wish my English was better. I suppose I will have to get the whole of this stuff translated. King Kong might be important.'

'I'm a busy man, Colonel, if you have no more questions . . .'

'No more questions. Only a bit of advice, Señor Quigly. With the signing of the Canal Treaty only a few weeks ahead we are anxious, as I told you, not to have any embarrassments. It's true you are not an American citizen, but you know how difficult the Senate in Washington can be. They would be only too willing to find an excuse to sabotage the Treaty and their own President. So I have a favour to ask you. For your own safety as well as ours be good enough to pack up your suitcase and walk across the Avenue of Martyrs and enter what is still the United States. Otherwise my colleagues might think something ought to be arranged – I mean of course an accident.'

Colonel Martínez gave an almost inaudible sigh of relief as Mr Quigly rose to leave without argument. He knew well that Mr Quigly was not a man of courage.

(2)

When Mr Quigly had gone, Colonel Martínez called for the translator and settled himself again at his desk to study the pages of the manuscript, seeking in them for a clue to three questions – on whose orders had Mr Smith taken the wrong direction with his arms, to Managua instead of to the north, and where was his son now and why had the son left behind this long manuscript? (The name Baxter persisted in escaping his memory.) The young man had known that Pablo was on his way to fetch him. Had he therefore intended Pablo to find the papers in the basket where he had, perhaps purposely, discarded them? The last part of the translation which began with an account of the boy's arrival in Panama was the only part which interested him. Even with his poor English, when he had glanced at the original, he understood enough to realize that the main interest must lie in his contacts with the man Quigly. The papers were rather like the notes resulting from a long self-interrogation, and the strange name King Kong had immediately caught his eye. Now he had before him the full translation of this last part in Spanish. On the surface it answered none of his questions, and Señor Quigly could not have been expected to identify King Kong. He had talked about a monkey or a gorilla. Perhaps that was a little joke, though Señor Quigly was not a man given to humour.

A knock on the door aroused him. Pablo entered and saluted. 'We have traced him, sir,' he said.

'Who?'

'Baxter.' Pablo had a better memory for foreign names than he.

'Is he alive?'

'He's alive. After he got his visa he booked a seat on a plane to Valparaiso, changing at Santiago.'

'Valparaiso? What an odd thing to do. Chile is no concern of ours – and his father had nothing to do with Chile, I'm sure of that – nor as far as we know had the man Quigly, though of course the Americans are in deep with Pinochet. But surely they would never send an amateur like that young man there. And yet he got his visa without difficulty. I wonder if we should let Señor Quigly stay?' He hesitated only a moment. 'No, I'm glad to be rid of him. It's just possible that their next financial correspondent will be an easier man to work against. All the same why Valparaiso?'

He touched the papers piled on his desk as though the mere feel of them might convey some answer to his question and then he spoke his thoughts aloud: 'King Kong. It haunts me that name King Kong. King Kong is the only clue we have. Could he be a name in some elementary book code which is all they would have trusted to an amateur like that? A character in Shakespeare perhaps. Some famous line that even the gringos would recognize. Well, the boy's gone. He can do no harm to us. All the same . . . how I would like to break that code of his. King Kong.' Colonel Martínez almost sang the name.

'I am no expert, but can it be that we have a clue there to the code word Quigly may be using in all the telegrams he sends to his newspaper? We have a lot of them on file. In any case this manuscript is worth preserving. One day it might well be of use to have it published to the world. In case after the Canal Treaty has been safely signed, we need to expose Señor Quigly and his gringo employers when they try to break their agreement, as they certainly will.' An idea struck him and he gave a little laugh. 'What a surprise for the boy if he were to see his book published in Spanish. Who knows it might even win a Cuban Prize for the best work on gringo espionage.'

The idea of the Cuban Prize pleased his humour so much that he ignored the telephone when it rang.

'I am sure if the General recommended the book to Fidel . . . oh, damn the thing . . .' He lifted the receiver and his face clouded. He rang off and sat a moment in silence. Then he told the translator in a tone of sadness, 'The son has followed the father.'

'But the father's dead.'

'So is the son. He will never see Valparaiso. An accident on the way to the airport. If it was really an accident, which I doubt. It is all the more important that you go on with the translation however irrelevant the earlier parts may seem. The vital question remains – what or who is King Kong?'

FOR THE BEST IN PAPERBACKS, LOOK FOR THE 🐧

In every corner of the world, on every subject under the sun, Penguin represents quality and variety—the very best in publishing today.

For complete information about books available from Penguin—including Puffins, Penguin Classics, and Arkana—and how to order them, write to us at the appropriate address below. Please note that for copyright reasons the selection of books varies from country to country.

In the United Kingdom: Please write to *Dept. JC, Penguin Books Ltd, FREEPOST, West Drayton, Middlesex UB7 0BR.*

If you have any difficulty in obtaining a title, please send your order with the correct money, plus ten percent for postage and packaging, to *P.O. Box No. 11, West Drayton, Middlesex UB7 0BR*

In the United States: Please write to *Consumer Sales, Penguin USA, P.O. Box 999, Dept. 17109, Bergenfield, New Jersey 07621-0120.* VISA and MasterCard holders call 1-800-253-6476 to order all Penguin titles

In Canada: Please write to *Penguin Books Canada Ltd, 10 Alcorn Avenue, Suite 300, Toronto, Ontario M4V 3B2*

In Australia: Please write to *Penguin Books Australia Ltd, P.O. Box 257, Ringwood, Victoria 3134*

In New Zealand: Please write to *Penguin Books (NZ) Ltd, Private Bag 102902, North Shore Mail Centre, Auckland 10*

In India: Please write to *Penguin Books India Pvt Ltd, 706 Eros Apartments, 56 Nehru Place, New Delhi 110 019*

In the Netherlands: Please write to *Penguin Books Netherlands bv, Postbus 3507, NL-1001 AH Amsterdam*

In Germany: Please write to *Penguin Books Deutschland GmbH, Metzlerstrasse 26, 60594 Frankfurt am Main*

In Spain: Please write to *Penguin Books S. A., Bravo Murillo 19, 1° B, 28015 Madrid*

In Italy: Please write to *Penguin Italia s.r.l., Via Felice Casati 20, I-20124 Milano*

In France: Please write to *Penguin France S. A., 17 rue Lejeune, F-31000 Toulouse*

In Japan: Please write to *Penguin Books Japan, Ishikiribashi Building, 2-5-4, Suido, Bunkyo-ku, Tokyo 112*

In Greece: Please write to *Penguin Hellas Ltd, Dimocritou 3, GR-106 71 Athens*

In South Africa: Please write to *Longman Penguin Southern Africa (Pty) Ltd, Private Bag X08, Bertsham 2013*

Printed in the United States
by Baker & Taylor Publisher Services